MW01171927

Edited 4/2014
First print 7/2014

ISBN# 1502483580

BOOKSTORE DISTRIBUTION

Createspace / Amazon.com

First and foremost, I would like to dedicate this book to my father Dennis Kordell. I know you're smiling down on my sister and I from heaven. We'll always miss you Cool Moe D!

To my precious grandmother. You were good to me when I wasn't even good to myself. And to my mother, you held me and my son down while I was on vacation. The true definition of a rider. Love you.

To my sister Mary, son Natavion, Nieces Sandra and Catherine, I love you dearly. To my cousin Toriano, AKA Sweet Tee thanks. Deasha and I'man, Zona, Tony, Doris, Jesse, Camilla, Julia, and the rest of the family and my friends, I appreciate you.

If I missed you, fill you name in the blank_____. To my people on lockdown. Just remember that Jah loves you. I want to give a special thanks to the surrounding cities. Winston-Salem, Greensboro, and last but not least, High Point. And any other city i missed just fill in the blank.

Love you,

Man.

Get It In
CHAPTER: One

Kesha knocked on Imf's door. She had already called him earlier that day to see if he was straight. Call her simple, but she only dealt with Imf on the coke tip cause his product was always A-One, plus he'd always looked out, gave her deals of some sort, and he never gave her anything she couldn't move. As she stood waiting on the other side of the door, she was deep in thought. Suddenly, Stack's snatched it open.

"Hey Stack's. Is Imf here?" She asked, as she peered around him.

"Yeah, come in." As Kesha eased past him in her tight low cut jeans, he eyed her incredible figure. *Damn, how did she fit all that ass in them jeans*, he wondered, shutting the door behind him.

"Yo Kesha. What's up?" Stack's questioned, rubbing his hands together.

"The rent," she shot back. *No. Stack's ain't tryna holler,* she thought. Stack's was cute, but she could tell he did more fronting and stunting then living up to his name. The last thing she needed was to be taking care of a grown ass man. She already had one of those at home, so an additional dependent was not an option.

Stack's smirked and stroked his beard with the palm of his hand.

"When you gonna get with the man. You know I can change your life," he flirted, letting his eyes scan her amazing curves in a tasteful manner.

"I'm pretty sure you would." *All to hell,* she said in the back of her mind. "Look stack's you know I already have a man," she broke things down as nicely as possible.

"Yeah," he replied. "So when you get ready for a boss let me know," he softly smiled, licking his lips as he groped his nut sack.

"You is crazy," she laughed, paying him no mind. "Where is Imf?"

"In there listening to that slow music," Stack's pointed, taking a seat on the sofa to finish playing his Playstation 3.

Kesha made her way to Imf's room, Jagged Edge's newest CD was playing. Imf had his shirt off, and was looking good as ever! As she cheesed, he pulled her into his embrace and spent her around like a princesses in a fairytale. Once he stopped, she ended up with her hands on his stout chest. Slowly, she lowered them around the smalls of his back.

"You want me to get at your B.M. (Baby Momma) for you?"

"How you know I'm going through it with my B.M." Imf chuckled.

"I always know when something's bothering you. So like I asked before, you want me to get at her for you," she sighed, brushing her lips against his earlobe. "Cause I will," she insisted.

"Nah, give her a pass," he laughed, right before he created some space between the two of them.

Sometimes just seeing Kesha made his whole day better. Shorty was a precious jewel. Too bad she already had a man. If it hadn't been for that, he would've locked shorty down a long time ago. Kesha was around 5 ft. 5 and resembled Lauren Hill of the Fugees. She was killin'em softly, and her 36-24-38, specks were a nice combination that would cause any brother to lust. Actually, her chocolate brown skin and hazel brown eyes only made her that much more exotic, which was also a feature that Imf loved. As his mind began to wander, he backed up. As he stared at her sexy lips, it was obvious that only the Lord knew what he was thinking.

Why did he have to have a B.M., and why do I have to have a man, she wondered to herself. *Shit is just complicated,* her mind fussed, making her feel frustrated.

"You know you not obligated to be with her just because y'all share a child together? All you gotta do is take care of your son," she informed him, sitting on his bed.

"Fo' show. Thanks for the heads up," he smiled, and so did she.

Imf was around 6 ft. 1, 201 pounds, with chocolate brown skin and thick long dreads that came down to his waist. While Kesha watched Imf weigh and bag up her work, she kept grinning at him. *Dang, he reminds me of the reggae artist Sizzla,* she thought, easing up off the bed to retrieve his money.

"I only got seven hundred. I owe you a hundred on the next go round," she told him.

"You good, Shorty." He took the seven hundred and didn't even count it.

"No, you gotta make your money," she complained. "You can't be taking no shorts."

"I ain't taking no shorts cause I know you gon' comeback and spend with me again."

"See, that's why I fucks wit' you. See you in a little while." She smiled, turning to walk out of the room.

* * *

Trick watched Kesha come out of Imf's building complex. Stupid ass Imf. *If he was that nigga, he would've been pushed up on a down ass bitch like Kesha,* he thought to himself. Not only was she one of the most exotic girls he'd ever laid eyes on, but she had a mean ass hustle game to go along with that.

"Sup, Kesha," he spoke as she got into her 2012 Altima.

"Hey, Trick," she waved.

"Hold up. You looking good in those jeans. How you get in 'em in the first place," Trick grabbed the door before she had a chance to close it. "Why you always dealing with Imf. I'm the real boss around here," he lied.

"I just do," she sternly replied, leaving it at that. "Now, if you'll excuse me?" She shut her door. "I really have to get going.....See ya," she waved at Trick who was a cold hater.

Bitch. He thought as she pulled off. He would show Shorty who the real boss was someday. All he needed to do was figure out a way how.

"Hey, Trick," Crackhead Amber opened the door to her apartment.

She had on a tight tank top that had her nickel sized nipples poking out. Amber was fresh on the pipe, which meant she hadn't lost her plump behind and good looks yet.

"What you want." Trick already knew she wanted some dope. He only hoped she was in desperate need, so he could trim her.

"Come in," she motioned for him to enter her house. Once inside, she shut the door behind them.

"What up?" asked a curious Trick.

"I need something for ten," she reached in her bra and pulled out a wrinkled up ten dollar bill.

Looking at how perky her breast was had his dick harder than a mu'fucker. Seemed like Shorty was tryna entice him with her big head lights.

"You know I only got twenties and up."

Amber sucked her teeth.

"Umm! You know I'm good for it," she confirmed.

"You know if I look out for you then I gotta look out for the whole hood," he stated.

"Come on, Trick. Just this once," she said pouting.

"Shit! You know the drill; no gwop, no rock!

Why was this nigga trippin? Amber asked herself, knowing she needed a hit something terrible.

"Come on, Trick. I promise to pay you by tomorrow night."

Trick stroked his goatee like he was in deep thought, which made Amber impatient and jittery.

"Come on, Trick. You know I don't deal wit' nobody but you," she poked her lips out.

"If I look out for you, what you gon' do for me?" He asked, grasping his throbbing dick. "You gone have to suck me off or something," he said, trying to persuade her.

Disgusting, she thought.

"I don't get down like that," she fussed totally shocked that Trick had the audacity to come at her like a crackhead. In her mind, she was far from a crackhead, considering that she was an occasional smoker.

"No." Trick crammed a big bag of rocks in the side of his jean pockets. "See ya."

"Hold up, Trick. Maybe we can work something out," she changed her tune. "I need a blast first."

"You can get a blast after I blast you." Trick unbuckled his pants and let his jeans drop to the floor.

Oh God, Amber thought, looking at Tricks stout elephant trunk. "I can't," she said, second guessing herself.

As if to almost read her mind. Tricks spoke up.

"I promise to look out for you," he pulled Amber into his

masculine chest.

"I'm not sucking your dick," she frowned.

"Cool. Just bend over," Trick suggested, turning her around. He slowly slid both hands underneath her shirt, and lifted her bra to toy with her nipples. Without waiting another minute, he started making love to her.

"Come on, Trick. Hurry up," she said, hiking up her skirt.

Trick used his hand to finger tease her frizzy pussy lips for a minute. Then he rubbed his dick head against her entrance without sticking it in. Amber got frustrated with all the four play and ended up slipping Trick into her wet entrance herself. With the way he was teasing her, she was dying to have him inside of her. As she eased him into her tight slit inches at a time, she cried out in pain.

"Damn you got a big dick, boy," she said with him halfway in.

"I know," Trick said before bending a standing Amber over to hit it from the back.

He held her hips and let her wildly ride him as his penis barely did any work at all. Deep inside of her, he just let Amber take all that he had to offer.

"Oh God." Amber held her erect nipples and thrust her hips back towards him. She was praying Trick didn't bust out of her. "Shit," she whispered, biting down on her bottom lip as he plowed in and out of her causing her pussy make a smacking sound. "Oh God," she moaned.

Kesha was so engrossed in their session that she grabbed his nut sack and matched his energy. She tried crawling away but he was right behind her, fucking her across the floor until she ended up on the couch. Trick busted a nut right inside of Amber and kept on stroking. He fucked her so good, she passed out on the sofa. He left her a gram on the living room table and eased out the house unnoticed.

Happy Hill Projects was over three thousand tenants strong. The Hills was one of the fiercest projects in all of Winston Salem, N.C.

Trick pulled a pack of New Port 100's out his pocket and tapped the pack to retrieve a loosy. He lit the C. I. with his lighter while thinking, *If I don't get out the P.J.'s soon, I'll just be another victim of the ghetto.*

"Trick, can you buy us some ice cream?" A little nappy headed kid asked with a bunch of other nappy headed project kids with him.

"Yeah, Trick," the gang of kids cosigned in unison.

"Hell no, I ain't y'alls daddy," Trick fussed, inhaling his cigarette.

"Fuck you. At least I know who my daddy is," snapped one of the little nappy headed boys as he took off with his entourage.

Trick shook his head. *Out of the twelve nappy headed mu'fuckers, none of they bad asses gon' make it in life. Six gon' get shot,* he thought, *and the other six gon' be crackheads like they crackhead mamas.*

"That's a damn shame," he uttered.

* * *

Kesha couldn't believe she was back at Imf's spot about to re-up again. She could've waited until tomorrow, but something about him being halfway naked earlier that day kept replaying in her mind. She knocked on the door to Imf's spot and Tank answered.

Tank was 6 ft. 5 and the size of a NFL linebacker. He was also one of the two henchmen Imf had on his payroll.

"What's up, Tank. Where's Imf," she asked.

"He in the backroom," Tank told her, shutting the door behind them. "But he kinda busy," he smirked.

"Busy!" She repeated, mocking what he'd just said. Imf was never too busy to get money. "Tell him I'm out here."

"No can do. He told me he wasn't having no dealings," Tank expressed, only doing what he was told.

"I don't have time for games," Kesha fussed, jetting past Tank's 275 pound frame to go knock on Imf's door. She giggled as Tank gave chase. He was too late.

"I told you he wasn't having no dealings, Kesha!" Tank yelled.

"What you gonna do, Tank, beat me up? I know I didn't hear no moaning," she asked, with attitude as her Negro intuition kicked in and she reached for the door knob.

"No Kesha!" Tank yelled louder, quickly pulling Imf's bedroom door back shut.

Damn. A nigga can't even get it in, he thought as he pulled up out of a bitch named Tip and got out of bed. "Tank and Big Timer can't hold shit down," he mumbled to himself.

"What you doing?" Tip wrapped her arms around Imf as he put on his pants. "You better finish what you started," she said, kissing on his neck.

"Hold it tight. Let me see what's going on right fast," he replied, smacking her on her round ass.

Tip was hot Imf was pushing her to the side like he was. What could be more important than her at this moment?

"If you don't get back in bed I'm bouncing," she told him.

Who this bitch think she giving ultimatums, he thought, leaving her butt naked on the bed to make his way across the room.

Once he reached the bedroom door, he yanked it open and saw Kesha.

He hiked his pants up to his waist, stepped out of the room and shut the door behind him.

"You busy. I could come back tomorrow," Kesha asked, peering in the room.

He looked at Tank, thinking, *how did a 130 pound woman get by a three hundred pound man.* Baffled, he had to asked.

"Yo Son, how you let her get by you? She sweet talked you or something?" He barked. "I thought I specifically told you I wasn't having no dealings," he went on to say. "I don't know what I pay you and Big Timer for. I might as well fire y'all and just watch out for myself."

"Imf!" Tank tried explaining.

"Don't cut me off, you through."

Tank took a deep swallow, turned and ice-grilled Kesha. "Thanks a lot Shorty."

"He's not about to fire you," Kesha spoke up, noticing that Imf raised an eyebrow as she talked.

"Yeah. You heard me," she told Imf, speaking on Tank's behalf. "He told me you wasn't having any dealings. But I really needed to re-up, so I kind of ran by him," she admitted.

Imf shook his head habitually. Kesha had a vicious hustle game. It was one o'clock in the morning and she was reing-up again.

"Um." Tip said, frowning after entering the room they were in. Upset, she sucked her teeth at Kesha because Imf was talking to her. "Skank," she smirked, snatching the door open to start out of the house.

"Your mama, Hoe!" Kesha really wanted to push home girl's buttons so she could have a good reason to whoop her ass.

"What you say, bitch?" Tip turned back around.

"If you want some then you can hear," Kesha spat, sitting her Gucci bag down on the sofa.

Tip rolled her eyes. She should've brought her girls with her.

They were more of the fighting type than she was.

"To bad you gonna miss out on this," she sassed to Imf, tracing her nice curves with her hand. "I don't know why I wasted my time with you," she remarked.

"He's only missing out on catching fleas," Kesha spat.

"Um," Tip clenched her teeth, looking Kesha up and down, before going out the door.

"You need to check your heffa's," Kesha snapped, looking at Imf who wasn't looking so sexy to her now, even though he was half naked with his shirt off.

"Damn, Kesha. It's one o'clock." *What a fucked up night*, he contemplated.

"M.O.B. Money Over Bitches," she told him. "You must be feeling that heffa," she teased, confident in her assumption that he really was.

"Kesha," he rubbed his temples.

What! No more Kesh, she thought to herself, which was the nickname he usually called her up to this point.

"I need two ounces. I got sixteen hundred, plus that extra hundred I owe you."

She thought money would make him smile, but it didn't, which meant he had to have really liked that heffa that left.

"Damn Kesh. You better be glad I fucks wit' you," he told her, heading to his room to get her the two ounces. Still pissed when he came back, Kesha knew she had to say something.

"I'm sorry Imf, I should've just waited until tomorrow to get at you," she said, apologizing for messing up his grove with the jump off. "If she really means that much to you, call her back," she suggested, placing the money in his hand before leaving.

"Man, I think she likes you," Tank said, after she was gone.

"Let me do the thinking," Imf said.

Instead of making some real paper, Tank's ass was supposed to be working at the Burger joint. Imf could understand why Tank liked Kesha, because she had just saved his job.

CHAPTER: Two

KESHA,

Lately I've been depressed. Not only was she PMSing. But her boyfriend Silk was on her case about moving some of his work. Silk was around 5 ft. 9, 175 pounds with an almond complexion. He resembled the actor/writer, Hill Harper. She and Silk had been together for almost two years. They went through their share of problems, but lately things had been getting out of hand. She wasn't in the mood for yet another argument, so when Silk got in the bed and started groping her, she put a stop to his progress.

"I hate to break the bomb shell on you, but my period came on today."

"You can still bless me with some skully," Silk replied, before nibbling at her neck.

Her face cringed up at him.

"I told you I don't feel comfortable sucking your thingy not knowing where it's been."

Silk never got caught cheating, but who's to say he wasn't.

"The only person I'm fucking is you." He couldn't believe Kesha.

He was loyal to her and busted his ass to make sure she had everything and anything she wanted. He knew what her attitude was about, it was Imf's punk ass. He got out of bed and tossed his clothes back on.

"Where you going?" Kesha inquired.

"The fuck up outta here!" He griped.

Silk knew it was a damn shame she was making another nigga money and not him.

Kesha could have stopped him from leaving but she chose not to. *If he wants to act up and have temper tantrums. Then let him,* she thought. She wasn't sucking his dick. Who did he think he was demanding shit from? She took care of him and not vice verse. *Let him leave.* She thought as he left.

* * *

Since Silk was acting like a bitch and hadn't been home for a few days, Kesha decided to get out and enjoy herself. She was dressed to impress. She had on a pair of Bottega Veneta skin tight denim jeans, a white top and Christian Louboutin heels. She wasn't rocking too much make up. Just a little eye liner and Mac lip gloss. She was with her girls Net and Angie. Net was only an eight or eight and a half. And Angie was kind of on the puffy side from eating way too many Twinkies and Milk-Duds. Angie was a soap opera hoe who had no real intentions on getting a job. She was a great booster and computer scam artist. Net on the other hand, she had the key to life.

She wasn't all that in the face, but it didn't make a difference, because once niggas got a glimpse of her round behind and spiraling curves, they got overwhelmed. And by then, she was working her hand. It was a well known fact that Net only dealt with niggas that were caked up. So if you wasn't caked up, then she wasn't even wasting her time.

Kesha, felt good about being with her girls. Lately her grind didn't allow her the time to kick it with them that much. Net was the first to hit the dance floor, so Kesha and Angie hit the bar to get a few drinks. On the way to the bar, they were surprised at who they saw.

"Gurl!" Angie said. "Ain't that your man?" She pointed her finger towards Silk and some high yellow chick all hugged up at a table together.

Before Kesha even knew it, she had spassed out, and was making her way towards Silk's table.

"Who is this Bitch? This is why you wanna break up? So you can fuck around?" She griped, lashing out at him.

Silk grabbed Kesha by her risk and twisted her arm behind her back.

"Tone that shit down," he yelled.

"Stop! You're hurting my arm," she struggled, but was no match for his strength.

"Get your ass in the car before I put my foot in your ass. You up in here acting all crazy and shit," He fussed, demanding that she move. Suddenly, he gave her a firm push in the back, forcing her body to go towards the exit.

She was lucky he didn't break her arm for getting all jazzy with him.

"Who this Bitch think she is?" He uttered to himself, glancing over at Net and Angie. He didn't know why Kesha associated with they sack chasing ass's. He also wished they would've gotten out of line, because he had no problem with smacking a hoe.

Kesha couldn't believe Silk embarrassed her the way that he did in front of her friends and the whole Forsyth County.

"This nigga done lost his mind," she mumbled to herself. As she waited by Silk's Range Rover, she wiped the tears from her eyes.

She wasn't even tripping about Silk practically ripping her arm off. All she kept thinking about was the girl she saw him with. *What's this niggas problem making me wait? Hell, it's starting to get cold out here.* She thought, caressing her arms as she waited on Silk's stupid ass.

Silk strolled to his SUV, used his remote to unlock the doors and crank up the Rover at the same time.

"Bitch!" he said, pressing his finger against her temple. "If you ever pull a stunt on me like that again, I will beat the day and night out your ass."

"Oh. You think you gangster now?" Kesha snapped, smacking the shit out of Silk's punk ass. "I can't believe you tryna shine on me," she spat and threw a fury of wild punches that barely missed him.

Kesha was a feisty little bitch, so Silk had to wrestle her to the ground. After he mounted on top of her, he smacked her head like it was a tennis ball and his hand was the racket.

CHAPTER: Three

Stack's slid a twenty dollar bill in the ass crack of a girl that looked half Asian and African American.

"Make that ass clap," he yelled, smacking her on the ass for motivation. "You rolling with a rider tonight?" He whispered in her ear.

"Why not just go to the Red light special?" She whispered back.

"What's the Red Light special?" Stack's asked, kind of new to this type of shit.

"Come on. Let me show you," she smiled, taking him by the hand.

* * *

"Can I give you a dance?" A girl asked Imf as he sat at the table with his gang.

She had been watching him ever since he came in the club and he seemed kind of laid back, so she took the initiative to see what a man as good looking as him was doing in such a sleazy atmosphere.

"Nah. I'm good Shorty," replied Imf.

"He said he's cool, Shorty," Big Timer told her, standing up.

"Who you, his body guard or something?" She snarled at him.

"He said he was cool," Tank repeated, taking a sip of his Ace of Spades. *Damn Groupies,* he thought.

She placed her hand on her hips in frustration.

"You know what?" She sucked her teeth.

"What?" Tank shot back really not wanting to smack a hoe tonight, but Shorty was taking the groupie thing a little too far.

"I'm pretty sure y'all run women off on the daily," she said, before she walked off.

She was due on stage at any minute. She went to the dressing room and changed into the colors of Ethiopia. As her name was being called, she slipped on her thick wedged heels. It was show time.

"Ladies and gentlemen, I would like to welcome to the stage, Exotic... And that she is," DJ KO replied, liking what he saw. As he stared at the new girl, he set the tone with a little Keith Sweat.

Maliah glided up and down the pole with so much grace that the stage was filled with cash. She had everyone's attention, except for the dark skin cutie with the long dreads and his two protectors.

She glimpsed over at him and couldn't tell if he had peeped her or not because he had on thick white Louis Vuitton shades. She raked all her earnings into her Crown Royal bag and made her way over to the dark skin cutie with the long dreads. As she approached, she shoved one of his two 300 pound fences back into their chair. The crowd went wild.

Big Timer didn't feel like the 6 ft. 7, two- hundred-fifty pound man he actually was. Okay, maybe two-hundred-eighty or more like three-fifty, but whatever it was, he felt small, like a half a centimeter.

Maliah realized she had Imf's attention now. She removed his shades and placed them on her instead. It's like they were the only two in the club that really mattered at this point. She straddled him as Silk's *Feel Like Loving Me* came on. Their physical chemistry was crazy. She could feel his temperature rising. *Yep. He's definitely into me;* she concluded as the swell in his pants increased. She rotated her hips and did a slow grind that had him nearly pop out his pants. *Too bad the song's over but,* she pondered to herself, browsing at him one last time before leaving to get dressed.

As Imf, Tank, and Big Timer chilled at their table, a waitress approached.

"This was sent to you gentleman," she expressed, sitting a bottle of Ace of Spades on their table.

"Yo, who the fuck sent this? I know these niggas ain't hating," Tank said as he watched her walk away. Sensing a need to be cautious, he pounded his knuckles into his fist and looked around the club.

"Calm down," replied Maliah."Gosh! I sent it. I noticed y'all were drinking Ace of Spades, so I sent y'all a bottle." Still taken by Imf's sex appeal, she looked him over once again. "Can I holler at you without your crew?"

Shorty was like that. She was wearing a black Marc Jacob dress with strap up stilettos. *She favors Trya Banks,* Imf rose from his seat very engrossed in his thoughts.

"Y'all good," he asked, placing his hand on Tanks shoulder.

"I got this," Tank said.

"Y'all go find out where Stacks is," Imf suggested.

"Can you walk me to my car?" Maliah asked. "Fo'show. Let's roll," he shot back.

***

Stack's walked out the Red Light Special after blasting the sexy bi-racial chick named Vita.

"We been looking all over for you," Big Timer said, happy they finally found Stack's. The lil nigga was always into some shit. Yet, they made it out the club tonight.

"Damn, Casanova," Stack's teased, watching Imf as he spoke with the fly shorty driving a BMW 745 Li.

He unlocked his doors to his Dark Blue Escalade and they got in. He started the ride and drove over to Imf while he got at Shorty. When he got in the ride, Stack's looked over at Imf.

"Whose ride she driving. I bet her niggas," Stacks inquired.

"I don't even care," Imf kinda chuckled. "Cause if she give me that ass then you know somebody getting fucked!" He laughed. "Yo, ain't that Hay-Zeus over there?" He gestured.

"Hell yeah," Stack's squinted his eyes to get a better look.

Hay-Zeus was tired of niggas playing games with his money. This nigga Bobby had the nerve to tell him he wasn't paying him after he fronted him three grams of coke. Now to see the same nigga in the club making it rain sent a rage of anger through Hay-Zeus.

This nigga gone pay me in full, Hay-Zeus vowed to himself. *Would rather hit the strip club then pay me my money.* He couldn't understand the niggas of this day and time. *Would rather go to hell or heaven*, he told himself in his wistful thinking. It's like he was in some kinda daze until he saw Bobby coming out the strip club carefree. He ran up on him with the Ruger and made his ass pay.

"Boom, boom." The sound of shots rang out.

"Stupid mu'fucker tricking off my shit." Hay-Zeus dug into Bobby's pockets and pulled out what was his in the first place. *A damn shame.* He pondered. "I told you I would get my cash homie." Hay-Zeus gave Bobby a head shot that sent brain matter everywhere. "Mu'fucker. I don't give a damn about you, have my money, Mu'fucker." He spit on him. "Got blood on my brand new sneakers. You just won't learn will ya?" Hay-Zeus shot Bobby two more times in his chest to send him to rest.

"Yo. That nigga crazy," Stack's said, musingly, about to pull off.

Imf stopped him in the process.

"Go pick that nigga up." In the back of his mind, he was thinking. The world could use another killer.

"Get in." Tank held his hand out the window. "Give me your gun," he insisted once Hay-Zeus was in the SUV.

For a minute Hay-Zeus had zoned out. He could also hear sirens, as he passed his gun to his right.

"Yo. You Big Bise's brother, right," Imf asked. Big Bise had caught a string of bodies back in 1992 and was currently doing life in prison.

"Yeah," Hay-Zeus replied.

"That shit must run in the family," Imf reflected. "We gotta get you out of dodge. What was that shit about," Imf was skeptical.

"That nigga owed me a hundred and twenty bucks; that trick ass nigga won't get the chance to owe me no more." Hay-Zeus gritted his teeth into a mean mug.

This kid was a monster. Plus he was hungry. And it was no doubt that Imf wanted him on his team. Until shit died down, Imf got Stacks to let Big Timer and Tank use his ride to take Hay-Zeus to one of their getaway houses in V.A. Imf and Stacks got out the SUV and headed to the spot. As soon as they took the elevator and made it to their floor, they ran into Trick.

Trick is becoming a nuisance, Stack's smirked before uttering some words cause Trick was in their territory, which called for a beat down.

"Sneaky mu'fucker." Stack's uttered. "You short stopping our sells?" Stack's gritted, wanting to smack the shit out of Trick's monkey ass.

"Nah, Son. I'm coming from a bitch house," Trick remarked.

"I ain't your son, you bum mu'fucker," Stack's barked.

"What Bitch," he questioned, knowing damn well Trick was lying to him.

"Not none of your bitches," Trick retorted. He could see Stack's was in his damn feelings as usual. He had a reason to because they were fucking some of the same bitches off and on. Trick backed up as Stack's lunged at him.

"Due-Boy-Ass-Nigga. Don't let me catch you out of pocket," Trick hated Stacks.

Cause when you do, you catching a beat down, Stacks, he thought as he took off in an all out sprint. He hit the stairway as Imf and Stack's gave chase.

Stack's and Imf reached the first floor out of breath.

"Don't let me catch you around here again," Stack's yelled as Trick ran like a refugee.

Stack's hated Trick with a passion. It was disrespect to be on another clique's turf; especially hustling in front of somebody else's spot. Niggas died behind things of that nature. Trick may have gotten away this time, but next time, his ass was grass.

"Nigga faster than a crackhead," Stacks Stated as he watched Trick run. "Run Trick run." He uttered to himself.

CHAPTER: Four

Maliah,

It was hard not to keep thinking about Imf. She couldn't believe she was actually sweating a nigga. After the third ring a male's voice lingered through the phone.

"Yo! Speak."

"Is this Imf?" She looked at the crinkled piece of paper Imf had written his number on. They had exchanged numbers, but he never called, so she took the first step by calling him.

"Who is this?"

"Maliah," she replied.

"Oh, what's good?" Imf asked. He paused to handle some business.

"I'm really trying to see why you haven't bothered to call me?"

"I really been busy getting this paper," he responded, keeping it plain and simple.

Dope boy. She thought absently.

"Aint nothing wrong with that." She said, in response. "Hold up. I'm cooking, so I have to go check on this food," she told him. She checked her food and returned back to the phone."Sorry about that."

"What you burning up?" Imf asked.

"No you didn't," she giggled. "I can cook, so don't get it twisted." She clutched her teeth.

"When you gon' let me judge for myself?" Imf asked.

"One of these days, homeboy," she said, laughing as she thought, *it depends on if you acts right.*

"I'm kinda hungry. Why don't you bring me a plate and let me sample something?" He requested.

"You trying to work me already," she sassed, pretending like she wasn't dying to see him when in all actuality she was. Finally, she gave in. "Where you live at?"

"In Happy Hill Projects," he replied. "You still there?" He double checked.

"Yeah." *There is just no way I'm trying to be hanging around in that grave site.* She debated in her mind on whether or not she wanted to see Imf that bad.

Ain't no way Shorty gonna bring me something to eat, he figured. Soon as he said something about Happy Hill Projects. It's like Shorty got lock jaw. He still gave her the info just in case she wanted to come through.

Shit was live in the PJ's. Imf, Tank, Stack's, and Big Timer were chilling outside when a couple of weed puffing bitches walked up on them. Tina, Red and Kim were known for using their erotic behavior to play niggas for their exotic weed. These bitches could make empires crumble. They would fuck a nigga one day and fuck his best friend the next. It varied based on whoever had the weed for the day.

"What up Stacks? Roll up," requested Red.

She was the same color as Hennessey, 5 ft. 4 with a mango tone, chingy eyes and some round never ending curves.

"Yeah, Stacks," Tina cosigned.

Tina was a copper brass tone, 5 ft. 1 with small hips, big ass and tits, sexy lips and greenish eyes.

"Come on Stacks." Kim pressed her firm body up against his.

Kim resembled the super model, Selita Ebanks. Too bad she was so damn ghetto. She had an innocent look, but yet and still she could be dangerous behind that pretty face and fat ass. As she pressed up against his bulging dick, he had to remind himself of that. He had been tryna fuck Kim for a minute now, the only problem was, he had fucked Tina and Red on so many occasions that they probably poured salt on his name.

"Roll this up," Stack's through Kim a Dutch and a fat bag of that Cush.

"Y'all bitches always wanna smoke up somebody's reefer," Tank said, leaning back on his Navigator.

"Smokey and the Bandits." Big Timer laughed. "Y'all can smoke all Stacks' shit up but no poky no smoky." Big Timer said, thrusting his hips like a skier while hitting the slopes, but making reference to fucking.

"Nigga, please! Don't make me tell them how you was eating my pussy," Red said, reflecting on how often he did it.

"Don't make me tell everybody how I fucked you in every hole," Big Timer, snapped. *No this bitch didn't,* he thought, clenching his teeth. "While you at it, tell everybody how you fucked up that abortion money."

Red was supposed to get an abortion but instead went and got her hair and nails done. *Crazy bitch, I already told her I had three baby mommas and four seeds,* Big Timer thought, turning the tables on her.

As Big Timer and Red put their business all out in the streets, Imf shook his head. He found the shit hilarious, as he watched them continue to go at it.

Niggas can be so damn ignorant, Imf thought, getting up to take care of a couple customers while Red and Big Timer's debate got more heated.

"You dirty, stank ass nigga," Red said, all in Big Timer's grill, mushing him with the tip of her finger.

Big Timer smacked Red's hand away from his face. *Ah Hell Naw!, It's time to put this bitch in her place. I never would've fucked her if I'd known she was gonna turn around and be such a fucking headache.*

"You bummy smoked out bitch. I can't believe you tryna trap me off. What's your problem?" Big Timer said, believing he was the victim.

"Trapped off." Red rushed Big Timer. She swung until she punched him in his shit.

"You bitch," Big Timer, snarled.

He rubbed his bottom lip, tasting the blood that spilled from it. He grabbed Red by her neck with one hand and smacked the shit out of her with the other.

"Somebody stop him." Kim looked at Stacks, then Imf.

"I don't got nothing to do with that," Imf said. He turned his head and looked the other way. "I learned a long time ago not to get into other peoples affairs."

"Yo. Ain't that ole girl?" Stack's said, pointing to a black Beamer.

"Yeah. I think so," Imf's replied, as his cellular started buzzing. "Sup," he answered.

"Come get your food." Maliah said, as she waited in her car for Imf to approach.

"What they fighting for?" She asked, as a huge man shook a girl by her shoulders.

"Long story," Imf chuckled, then stood in front of the driver's side to peep Maliah's coco buttered thighs.

"Aren't you going to stop him?" She asked. "She sure could use some help." Maliah gave him a compromising glance.

"I don't get into other peoples squabbles."

"Please." She pleaded, placing her hand on top of his.

It's like Shorty could see through his soul right then.

"Wait here," he said, and then went over and broke shit up.

Seeing how easily Imf dissolved the situation, Maliah knew he had plenty of respect.

"Chill out Big Timer. That's enough," Imf said.

"I'm calling the cops, fool!" Red screamed, feeling humiliated.

This bitch got me fucked up, he thought, which forced him to speak up. "And I will beat they ass like I did you." Big Timer promised.

"Come on, gurl. You'll be alright. Fuck that nigga," Kim said, placing her arm around Red. "You know you can't call the police," she told Red.

"I know." Red sobbed, wiping the tears from her face. "I was just frustrated," she responded, looking at Big Timer. "I love you. How can you do me like this?" She shouted like a mad woman. "Come on, gurl."

As she became teary eyed, Kim gave her a shoulder to cry on. Red had made a costly mistake. She was officially dick whipped. There was no coming back after a nigga done piped you down good, and then cut you off. *Big Timer's kinda cute,* Kim thought as she escorted Red to her apartment.

"That was nice of you," Malia smiled as Imf came back to her car and got in on the passenger side. "I got your food in the back seat." She told him.

Imf grabbed the plate of food and the 20oz Coke from the back seat. He peeled the aluminum foil back to find barbecue chicken, green beans, yams and cornbread. As he ate, he moaned.

"See, you was doing all that hating," smiled Maliah. "Say you sorry," she replied, knowing she could cook her butt off. Something that was inevitable due to her southern roots.

"You a'ight?" Imf questioned, dabbing his mouth with a napkin.

She could see that he wasn't going to give credit where credit was due.

"Why your boys keep looking over here?" She commented, as they peered over at them at times.

"I don't know," Imf gave a shrug of the shoulders.

"They act like you Nino Brown or something," she commented. "Do you always have to be so protected?" She questioned.

"What you mean protected?" He snapped, thinking, *Shorty got me fucked up.*

She could see Imf took her comment the wrong way, so she felt she needed to clean things up.

"I mean, it's like every time I'm with you we're being watched. Can't you leave your post for a second?" She inquired.

"I can do whatever I want. What you got in mind?" He queried.

"You'll see," she smiled, starting the car to kidnap Imf away from his boys.

* * *

"Yo. Where they go?" Tank asked out loud. "I don't know, but Red got me 38 hot," Big Timer replied.

Stack's laughed.

"You got a buss down pregnant. Stupid ass nigga," he uttered.

"Fuck you, nigga," Big Timer snarled, not in the mood for Stack's shit.

He hated when Imf left Stack's in charge. Stack's wasn't qualified to hold things down, and too often he showed he couldn't handle problems well. Stack's was more of the shoot 'em up bang, bang type, whereas Imf was more of a thinker instead of all that gun play. Don't get it twisted, Imf could be a ticking time bomb if you pushed him to his limit. Sometimes you could kill niggas just by being humble; and that's what Imf was, humble. Like even when he killed niggas, he always managed to stay humble.

* * *

Maliah parked and took her keys out the ignition.

"You coming in with me. I gotta pay my phone bill," she said to Imf. "Come on."

Imf got out of the car and followed Maliah so she could pay her cellular bill. He admired the way her short gray gym shorts hugged her figure.

"You are cutting up," he said, getting the door for her.

"How I'm cutting up?" She wanted to know. "What I do?"

"You killin' 'em," Imf replied, groping his nut sack.

"You off the chain," she insisted, noticing a couple of guys mean mugging Imf.

"Damn," Imf mumbled, as Trick and his boys caught a whiff of him. *I sure hoped like hell I don't have to show my ass.*

"If it ain't Imf. You ain't shit without your homeboys, huh," Trick taunted still salty about Imf and Stack's chasing him the other night.

"Let's leave," Maliah said to Imf.

"Hell no! Not until you pay your phone bill." Imf insisted, nodding in the direction of the empty register.

"You better listen to your broad, before you end up in heaven," Trick warned.

"I won't be the only one," Imf replied. "Now go on and pay your bills," he told Maliah. "You need some gwop?"

Maliah looked at Imf. He wasn't scared one bit. As she went to pay her bill, she worried the entire time about him. Trying to avoid conflict, she paid her bill and walked back over to Imf.

"I'm ready."

"Don't worry about them cat's, they know how I get down," Imf assured her pulling Maliah into his embrace.

She could feel his bullet proof vest and his gun holster. She realized she should've been scared, but a part of her was turned the fuck on.

* * *

"You think that nigga was strapped?" Face asked Trick.

"Had to be, but yo, who was that bitch?" Trick asked Joe-Joe.

"I don't know, but that nigga show is lucky," Joe-Joe said without thinking.

"That nigga won't be lucky when I put one in his wig." Trick's blood boiled every time he thought about Imf's bitch ass.

"What that nigga do to you?" Rufus asked his leader.

Trick thought back to high school. He was scared to ask a girl named Tonya to the school prom, and when he did work up the nerve to do so, what happens?

"*Tonya,*" Trick said with his heart pounding like the Daytona 500.

"*Hey Thadious,*" Tonya faced him and gave him her undivided attention. "*The prom is almost here.*"

"*Yeah, I can't wait. I'm going with Ingram,*" she said like she was really excited.

Fuck Imf and that bitch, Trick thought. Last time he saw Tonya. She was fat as a house with 3 kids.

* * *

"You should've seen that nigga. He was hating like a city cop. I don't know what that nigga got against me," Imf said while he told

Stack's, Big Timer and Tank about what happened while he was with Maliah.

"Look at you. You made it and he didn't. From now on I'm not letting you out of my sight. You want me to take care of Trick," Tank asked Imf looking for the okay.

"Nah. Let him live," Imf said in response.

As he answered Tank his cell went off. He picked up to Hay-Zeus on the other end. The nigga was home sick, out of weed and broke. *Good* thought Imf. *The hungrier the better.*

"I got somebody on the way to pick you up now," he told Hay-Zeus.

* * *

Kesha sat at home on her couch, listening to *Foolish* by Ashanti. Foolish is what she was. Why did she put up with Silk's controlling ass? Especially, the way the nigga beat the hell out of her, and as of lately, Silk had been wilding out for no reason. He'd been forcing her to have sex with him when he wanted it and how he wanted it, mentally and physically abusing her, and then saying he was sorry, or it wouldn't happen again. She hated that fool.

Feeling overwhelmed, she picked up her phone and dialed Angie's number. Angie picked up on the first ring winded, and sounding as if she had been running.

"Hello," she answered, panting.

"What up, gurl?" Kesha asked.

"Sup gurl? You need me to get Crazy and Gutter over there?" Angie questioned.

"No," Kesha quickly said. Crazy and Gutter were Angie's brothers. They specialized in beating the crap out of people.

"Umm!" Angie said, sucking her teeth.

Silk needed his ass whooped.

"You need to leave Silk. What happened to that fine ass nigga that looked like Sizzla Kalonji?" Angie inquired.

"Imf? He got a baby momma, and a few other chicken heads on the side," she replied, immediately thinking about the disrespectful bitch she had the encounter with the last time she went to re-up.

"I don't care about his baby momma or none of them other bitches, 'cause once he get some of Angie, he won't be thinking about them half starved bitches."

"You's a mess," Kesha told Angie, smiling.

Angie had a mean swagger, but on the real, she gave herself more credit than anyone else would.

"You the mess," Angie said to Kesha. "And you need to give me Imf's number if you ain't gon' put it to use."

"I am not about to give you Imf's number," Kesha responded and Angie knew that. So why she even ask, Kesha had no idea.

"Hater!" Angie laughed. "You just scared he might like what he see." Angie sucked her teeth.

"I'm scared you gon' get my connect locked up for computer fraud," Kesha burst out laughing.

"No you didn't. I'm not feeling your jokes," Angie frowned.

"I ain't feeling you tryna push up on my connect either."

"You need to share. He probably got enough dick for both of us," Angie teased.

Kesha frinzed, not even wanting to comment, yet she couldn't resist.

"You too much. What you smoking on?"

"Nothing, I need some exotic, cause I'm tired of smoking this Reggie Miller floating around," Angie informed Kesha. "Why don't you come and pick me up so we can go find some exotic Dro or Haze?"

"Give me about twenty minutes," Kesha said before hanging up.

After throwing on a white tank top, a short pair of coochie cutters and white air ones, and her thick hoop earrings with her name on them, Kesha left the house, and walked towards her Altima. Once she got to Angie's house, she had to wait over ten minutes in the driveway for her to bring her fat ass out.

"Hey gurl," Angie said, getting into the car.

Kesha looked over at Angie. She was wearing a light blue *Baby Phat* shirt with White Capri pants and strap up sandals. Angie could dress her ass off, and she had this stylish crop cut. Kesha smiled, *this girl has always rocked the toughest wardrobes and her hair has always been on point.*

"Where we going?" Kesha asked Angie.

"I hear they got that fire green in the Hills."

"Who got it?" Kesha looked over at her frowning.

"Somebody said Stack's got them," Angie answered.

Kesha started the car and drove to the Hills. As two police cars sat posted up, watching all the illegal activities in the area, they tried to conceal themselves as much as possible, so no one could see them. Aware of the surveillance being done in the area, Kesha parked and her and Angie got out of her car.

"Imf, don't y'all see the police over there in the cut? Kesha cut her eyes in the direction of the law enforcement.

"They just tryna get on the payroll," Stack's groped his dick as he scanned Kesha from head to toe.

"Yo nigga! You get distracted too easily," Imf said as he approached Kesha. He was having a hard time with distractions himself. "What you doing with them little ass shorts on." Imf asked Kesha.

"`Cause I'm grown and I can wear whatever I want," she replied.

"Don't get smart."Imf replied, realizing that he was molesting Kesha with his eyes.

"Hey, Imf," Angie waved.

Disgusting, Imf thought. Angie had a body like a Teddy bear. He didn't even acknowledge her. He was wondering why he hadn't seen Kesha.

"You ain't fucking wit' me no more?" He asked.

There was no way she was gonna tell Imf that she and Silk were going through their ups and downs.

"If it serves me correctly the last time I came through, you was pissed off at me."

"Oh, Tip," he said, stroking his beard with the palm of his hand and chuckling to himself.

"Yeah. That one" She replied. "I can't believe you was fucking that heffa. Straight buss down." She looked at him and shook her head in disgust, while she folded her arms across her chest. "I'm convinced you like easy women." She retorted.

"The easier the better." Imf slapped Stacks' hand with a high five for conformation.

"Ghetto ass niggas," she mumbled under her breath.

"Y'all got some exotic?" She asked Imf.

"Yeah." Imf pulled out a big bag of Purple Haze and a box of *Dutch Masters* and gave it to Kesha to roll up. "Can I holler at you right quick?" He asked.

A couple of things ran through Kesha's mind. *Maybe he was gonna tell her he had been thinking about her almost as much as she had been thinking about him.*

"What you got to holler at me about?" She asked Imf, following him into the staircase.

"How your money look?" He shot back.

"It's alright, I guess. I know I'm not ready to re-up yet."

She had only been selling to a selective few. Plus Silk was acting like a real piece of shit every time she left the house.

Imf took a deep sigh and leaned back on the wall.

"I need a favor," he said, easing his foot against the wall. "Nah. Never mind," he quickly changed his mind, knowing she would probably say no.

"No! Tell me! What is it?" She placed his hand in hers, hoping he was about to express how he felt about her. "Tell me."

"I need someone to drive me down to Texas. Imf let out a deep breath.

"And I guess that someone is me, right?" She glared at him still holding his hand.

"How do you do that?"

"What?" She smiled.

"I don't know. It's like you be reading a niggas mind or something," he told her. "So….. are you down?"

"Why me?" She let his hand go.

"Why not you?" He frowned, playfully shoving her.

"Why you always acting all hard?" She shoved him back.

"Cause I can," he chuckled.

"When you need me to drive you?"

"This weekend," he told her.

"Then I guess I'll catch you then," she started to walk off.

"Yo!" He called out.

"What," she turned around and noticed his eyes gazing at her.

"My weed." She smirked. "I almost forgot."

"Fire that shit up," he said, pulling the blunt from behind her ear.

"That weed you can have. But you gotta smoke one with me before you bounce." He lit the blunt and took a puff.

"So how that nigga of yours treating you?" He asked, blowing out a ring of smoke.

"Silk?" she replied.

"Yeah. I forgot." He passed the blunt her way.

"So everything's all good with the bills and shit? You ain't wanting for nothing is you?" He asked.

"No. I guess everything is good," she informed him.

"I see you ain't been to the hair shop in a while," he said. "Or the nail shop. And what's up with the shorts, tank top and Air Force Ones?"

"Why? You don't like the way I look?" She asked him, smiling.

"Nah, it ain't that. I'm just use to you being all glamed up."

"I know. You ain't gotta remind me. I haven't been on my grind like I should. But you know shit is gon' get better," she smiled.

"No doubt. Cause I'ma make sure that it is. You gon' get the rental car in your name?"

"It's whatever." She passed Imf the blunt.

"That's what I like to hear." He told her.

"I have to go," Kesha said, hearing Angie out front calling her name all crazy.

"Hold up," he stopped her.

"What?"

"Go pick up the whip and get your shit together." He tossed her a large stack of money.

Kesha flipped through the large roll of money.

"What's all this for," she asked Imf.

"I appreciate all the things you do for a nigga," he expressed to her.

Kesha wrapped her arms around Imf's neck and gave him a hug.

Silk who, he thought.

"Fuck that nigga," he said as he watched Kesha go get Angie and bounce.

* * *

It never dawned on Kesha to even ask Imf what the fuck they were going to Texas for. To tell the truth, she could have cared less. All she really wanted to do was get the chance to show Imf that she was a rider. She laughed to herself as she pulled up to Happy Hill in a black Yukon Jeep.

If Silk found out that she was going to Texas and not New York to visit her parents like she said, he was gonna definitely flip.

"Tank, can you tell Imf I'm out here?" She cut the music down.

"Word." Tank called out to Imf on his Motorola walkie talkie.

"Yo, Imf. Kesh out here."

"What's wrong with you, Big Tank?" Kesha noticed Tank wasn't his normal self.

"Nothing." Tank Lied.

"I'm leaving you in charge so hold things down," Imf said, coming down the steps with Stacks. "Don't fuck up," Imf advised Stacks.

"I got it." Stacks told Imf. "Yo. Just go on and have a good trip."

"Word." Imf dapped Stacks up while Big Timer carried his bags to the SUV and tossed them in the back.

"What's wrong with you?" Imf asked Tank.

"Take me with you," Tank said in a low tone, thinking about how he hated it when Imf left Stacks in charge.

"Please," Tank pleaded.

"No." Imf patted Tank on the back. "Watch out for my lil Cousin." Imf told him.

"Come on, Tank,." Stacks yelled. "I need you to go get me some blunts and cigarettes."

"See, Imf. That's the shit I'm talking about. I ain't no damn store man," Tank muttered. I'ma trained assassin."

"Come on, Tank," Stacks called out.

"See. This nigga sending me on store runs while I'm supposed to be protecting his stupid ass. You need to talk to that young nigga," Tank said as Stacks called him for the third time.

Imf could feel where Tank was coming from.

"Yo. Tank," Imf yelled out.

Tank turned around, hoping Imf was gonna let him roll with a player. His hopes were up.

"Yo," he answered.

"Watch out for my lil Cous," Imf insisted a second time.

"Word." Tank uttered, lowering his head in defeat.

"What's wrong with Tank?" Kesha asked.

"He don't wanna be left behind with Stacks," Imf said.

"I don't blame him."

"That is my cousin," he laughed.

"From one real nigga to another." She said with a grin.

"Yo. You know how much this shit gon' cost to fill up?" He asked in his reference to the Yukon.

"You told me to rent a car. You ain't say what kind." She laughed.

"You got that?" He leaned back in his seat.

"So," she paused.

"What?" He asked.

"Nothing," she sucked her teeth.

Imf shrugged his shoulders and rested back in the seat. Kesha drove in silence. She couldn't believe Imf didn't notice her new hairdo, even when she hinted to him. Niggas, she thought to herself.

Imf noticed Kesha was silent.

"Yo. Why you so upset?" He asked, leaning over.

"It don't even matter," she spat.

"You thought I didn't notice your hair?" He leaned back in his seat. "It looks good like that."

"You like it?"

"Yeah, but you can have that shit in a ponytail and I'll still say the same thing," he cracked the window a little.

"What you crack the window for?" Kesha asked, looking over at him and said.

"Take a smoke break." He lit a fat blunt then he and Kesha puffed on it and caught an serious high.

* * *

Meanwhile, Stacks was out front in the PJ's chilling with Hay-Zeus. He'd just made his return from Virginia.

"Yo! Ain't that Trick's little Cousin, Digga?" Stacks' asked.

"I don't know," Hay-Zeus said absent mindedly.

"Hell yeah! That nigga know better than to be around here. Let's go beat his ass."

Stack's and Hay-Zeus approached Digga and about three other niggas.

"Yo. Keep it moving," Stacks insisted, revealing his gun. "This the last time I'ma let you see it. Next time I catch y'all around here, I'm airing shit out and asking questions at the funeral." Stacks' found himself laughing at his own joke. "Punk mu'fuckers. Beat it," he demanded.

***

Of course Digga went and told his older cousin Trick. It didn't take long before Trick and his men were loading up their guns.

"I'm tired of these niggas thinking they run something. I should've taken these niggas out a long time ago," Trick said with anger. "Let's do this."

***

Trick and his men pulled up front of Imf's spot making niggas hop, skip and jump as they rode by in a dark SUV dumping fire.

***

It hadn't been ten minutes after Tank got from the store that he was leaping on top of Stacks and taking him to the ground for cover.

"Stay down," he told Stacks as shells flew over their head.

When the shots stopped ringing, Tank helped Stacks up off the ground and into the building they hustled out of.

"You alright?" He helped dust Stacks off. "What happened since I left?"

"I seen little Digga tryna eat around here, so I told that nigga to raise up," Stacks shared only telling half the truth. "I guess he went and told Trick some ole bullshit. I'm about to air that nigga out," Stacks said mad as hell.

"Cool down. For one, you know Trick is pussy. Which means he's not gonna be at the spot. And two, you know I gotta call Imf before we jump to any conclusions," Tank stated.

"Fuck that, pussy ass nigga," Stacks spassed. "Come on, Big Timer you and Hay-Zeus come with me," Stacks motioned.

"What about the money?" Tank asked Stacks.

"The money can wait. We can't make no money with niggas shooting up our spot," Stack's shot back, as he, Hay-Zeus and Big Timer climbed into his SUV. "Somebody about to die, my nigga."

Tank shook his head and got on the phone and called Imf.

* * *

Imf wasn't too excited about the news he'd just received from

Tank. Here they were not even out of Tennessee yet and Stacks was already wilding out.

He told Tank where to locate some product so he could take care of the steady flow of customers that Stacks was supposed to be taking care of. Frustrated, he took a deep sigh as he shut his cell.

"What's wrong?" Kesha asked.

"Nothing," he lied.

* * *

Stacks had been looking high and low for Trick's punk ass, but couldn't find him. So what he did was set a few examples. He stopped his SUV and hopped out the ride. He saw a nigga that hustled for Trick, so he pulled out his gun and pistol whipped the fool on site.

"Punk, Mu'fucker. Tell Trick he next." Smack, Smack, Smack!

Stacks bopped him with his chrome Glock 9, got back into his ride and sped off. As he drove, he saw a nigga driving Imf's baby's momma, Alexia's drop top CLK Mercedes.

"Fuck this shit," he muttered as he followed the nigga driving Alexia's whip. "This nigga think he gon' ride in a car my cousin paid for. Hell no!" Stacks said as the driver of the car came to a complete stop.

Stacks got out the ride with his gun drawn. The driver of the car must've sensed trouble, because he pressed down on the gas. Stacks aimed his gun sideways, trying to get at the nigga in the car.

"Get in," Hay-Zeus told Stacks. "Let's get that nigga," he suggested.

Stacks climbed into the whip, and ran the red light just like the driver of the car did. He drew down on the gas pedal, driving like a mad man.

"I'ma kill that nigga."

"You ain't catching that Mercedes," Big Timer stated.

"Oh yeah," Stacks retorted. "Check this." He pressed down on the gas pedal with everything he had, then hit a turbo button. "Dope Fiend Willie put this shit in," he told the crew as his whip road like the whip in "Back to the Future". Big Timer and Hay-Zeus held onto the door handle as Stacks maneuvered in and out of traffic.

J.T got on the phone and called up, Alexia.

"Yo, Bitch! Who are these wild ass niggas you got shooting at me?" He asked, looking in his rear view mirror. "What the fuck, never mind!" He hung up he couldn't believe that the SUV was right on his trail. "I thought I lost that nigga," he uttered before he was side swiped and sent into a ditch. He was surely a dead man.

"Yo! Ain't that Trick in that Durango Jeep?" Hay-Zeus asked, motioning with his hand as Stacks came to a halt.

"God was on his side," Stack's made reference of the nigga sporting Imf's B.M's car.

We got bigger fish to fry, he thought, switching routes to chase Trick, once again hitting the turbo button the Dope Fiend Willie put in. He started dumping fire, as did his boys. They laced Trick's ride up like a sewing machine, but somehow Trick got away.

"That nigga is a cold bitch," Stacks laughed along with the crew.

Hay-Zeus had a slight grin on his face.

"You crazy," he told Stacks. "What else you got on the agenda?"

"I got these chicken heads that need to get plucked. So we can all get fucked and sucked proper, I'ma call them and tell them to set it out." He got on his cell. "Yo. I got an order to put in," Stacks' said to the shorty he'd just called up.

* * *

Kesha and Imf were in Alabama when his cell started chirping nonstop.

"Yo." He answered.

"Stupid, mu'fucker. Why you trace my boyfriend and make him run off the road," Alexia snapped.

"Bitch! I'm out of town. Miss me with that bullshit," Imf spat.

"No! You miss me with that bullshit. You just mad cause I moved on with my life and it's over between us."

"Yeah. Whatever Bitch. How my son doing?" Imf changed the tone of his voice.

"He okay. I guess."

"Yo. You gon' let me slide through and smash when I get back while that nigga laid up in hospital?"

"That is not funny," Alexia laughed.

"It wasn't meant to be funny. I just wanna know if I can put this big boy in your life when I come through and see my son."

"I don't know, Imf. You know I got a man."

"And you can keep him. I just wanna give you what you really want."

"And what's that?" She puckered her lips.

"Pipe," he replied.

"You's a mess," she chuckled.

"So….. that means you down to get a room?" He found himself gripping his cock.

"We'll see when you get back."

"What you gon' tell your nigga."

"That I'm taking your son to see you for a few days. Don't worry. I got him."

"And I got you," he said before he hung up.

"Nasty ass nigga. Can you stop rubbing yourself," Kesha frowned.

"My bad," Imf chuckled.

"I see why you be having problems with your baby momma."

"Why?"

"Cause you keep fucking her and not wanting to be with her. That's wrong," Kesha said.

"That bitch ain't no good," Imf told Kesha.

"Then why you keep fucking her?"

"Cause she keeps fucking me."

Kesha got quiet.

"How so?" She asked.

"She climbs on top of me, and then I pipe her ass down," Imf chuckled.

"Stupid." She shoved his arm. "Here I believed your ass. Anyway, moving on, when we gonna pull over and get a room so I can get some sleep?"

"Maybe in a few," Imf said. "Pull over. I'll drive while you get some rest."

Kesha pulled over on the side of the highway and they switched seats. As Kesha got some shut eye. Imf called Stacks.

"Yo. Why the fuck you chase Alexia's boyfriend off the road for?"

"Fuck him. That nigga was driving the car you paid for around the city, so you know I pulled up on him. I didn't smack him up or nothing," Stacks' boasted. "Just ran his bitch ass off the road," he indulged in a light chuckle.

"You crazy, boy! So, I hear Trick and them got at you," Imf replied.

"Yeah. But it was nothing. We got back at them toy gangsters. It's hard to stay sucker free in the land of lollipops. So what's good with you and Kesh. You plan on hitting that?" Stack's asked. "I know I would."

"Nah. Business before pleasure," Imf muttered.

"You better than me." Stack's told the truth for once. "I know if it was me, I would eat that pussy like the last supper."

"Crazy ass-nigga," Imf laughed.

"What she up to?" Stacks asked.

"Sleep. Why?"

"Grab that ass for me," Stacks teased.

"Freaky ass nigga," Spat Imf. "But yo, stay out of trouble until I get back. Can you do that?" Imf asked.

"Yeah." Stacks replied.

Imf got off the phone. He was tired, so he pulled over at the nearest hotel. He tapped Kesha to wake her.

"Yo. I need you to go grab us two rooms," he said.

Kesha yarned and stretched out. Then went and copped the both of them a room. She went to her room and took a nice long shower.

Imf went in his room and did the same. He was wondering what ever happened to Maliah, as he dried off and tossed on his briefs and gym shorts. After he rolled up a blunt and laid back in bed, he blew big rings of smoke. Suddenly, there was a knock at his door.

"Yo." Imf barked. "Who is it?"

"Me. Kesha."

"What you want?" He asked as he pulled the door ajar and scanned Kesha's body.

"I'm bored," she said, stepping into his room. "I'ma chill with you," she told him, making her way to the bed.

Imf's private got erect. He shut the door and made his way to the bed as well.

"Why you not tryna get some rest?"

"I tried too. I can't sleep, so I must've slept good in the car," she said.

"Make yourself at home," Imf said, watching as she flopped on his bed. He passed her the blunt as his cell started buzzing.

"Yo," he said, answering. Once he heard the sound of Maliah's voice, he smiled. "What's good, Maliah?"

Kesha contorted her facial expressing, as she watched Imf talked on the phone. He placed his finger over his mouth, signaling her to stay quiet. She sucked her teeth and muttered under her breath.

"Heffah."

"Who was that?" Maliah asked.

"Nobody," Imf replied.

"Excuse me!" Kesha spoke up.

"Hold for a second," Imf covered the mouth piece of the phone. "Yo, this shit's important."

"And I aint?" She muttered.

"Like I was saying," Imf replied, continuing to talk to Maliah.

He got off the bed and made his way out the room.

"I'm O.T. right now, but when I get back. We definitely gotta kick it. So, how come I'm just now hearing from you?"

"Well," she said. "I been O.T too."

"Where you been?"

"Brazil."

"Damn girl. What the fuck you been doing in Brazil?"

"A photo shot."

"I definitely gotta check that out," he teased. "Did you miss me at all?"

"Of course. I can't wait until you get back," she informed him.

"I can't wait to get back either," he smiled.

Kesha walked out the door and shoved him out of her way. *What's her problem, h*e wondered, getting off the phone with Maliah to go to Kesha's room. He wanted to see what was up with her.

"Hold up," Kesha told Silk. "My little brother at the door." She lied.

She popped the door open and shushed Imf the same exact way he did her.

"Yeah, baby. I miss you. You don't even have to ask," she blushed. "I can't wait until I get home either." She giggled, noticing a frown on Imf's face. *Now you know how it feels, s*he told herself. *That shit hurts, don't it,* her mind screamed. "Yeah, Silk I just want us to work on getting things back how they used to be. I'm tired of all the arguing and fighting we been doing lately. Some changes definitely have to be made," she huffed. "So how is everything at home?"

"Good. When can I expect you back?" Silk questioned, because he he had a string of bitches he needed to slay before Kesha got back.

"I don't know," she responded. "You just behave yourself."

"Alright. You do the same," he shot back before he hung up.

Damn. No goodbyes, no I love you, she thought as Silk hung up.

"Damn! That nigga too gangster to say I love you?" Imf smirked.

"Shut up." She peevishly said.

"See. If that nigga had any sense, he would give you what you want," Imf continued to laugh.

"And what's that?" She retorted.

"Can't say," he answered, thinking *Me.*

"Then why bring it up," she snapped. "And how long have you been seeing Maliah?"

"Why?"

"Cause! It seems like you're really into her. Are you?"

"I'm into a lot of broads who giving it up."

"Y'all fuck yet?"

"Not yet."

"But y'all will," she prematurely answered for him. "It ain't hard to tell," she commented. "And you need to be careful."

"I'ma protect myself."

"I would hate to have to whoop that bitches ass if she hurt you," she frowned. "Cause when it comes to women; you don't have a clue," she assured him. "And patience is a virtue."

"Patience is something I don't have. But yo, anyways, I'm about to get some sleep. Do you need anything?" He asked, glaring at his watch.

"No. Get some sleep."

* * *

Imf and Kesha reached Dallas, Texas. Kesha drove on a pleasant quite street, and pulled into the driveway of a nice brick home to park. As they waited in the driveway, a dark complexioned man emerged from the house. He looked Jamaican, but to Kesha's surprise, he was of Spanish decent.

"Pamana," Imf greeted, hopping out the car to dap his long time associate up with a hand shake.

"Hey, Bro." Panama glimpsed into the SUV at the beautiful lady with Imf. "Who's she, your new wife?"

"Nah," Replied Imf. "That's Kesha. She's a good friend."

"She's beautiful," Panama waved.

Kesha returned the gesture.

"Let's take a walk," Panama suggested to Imf. "Mona." He called for his wife. When she came to the door, Panama requested that she show Kesha around the house while him and Imf talked. "So, this Kesha," Panama said with a slight grin on his face.

"What about her?" Imf chuckled.

"You bag her yet?"

"Na."

"What's taking you so long?" Panama asked.

"Shit's complicated."

"How so?"

"For one, she has a man."

"Hold it," Panama cut him off. "Best believe me, if the shoe was on the other foot her man wouldn't give a damn about you." Panama warned Imf. "Plus, anything worth having is worth taking. Always remember what I just told you. She means a lot to you. I feel that. You're worried about the money and business aspect," Panama stated, as if he had read Imf's mind. "But the truth is. You and Kesha shine together. I can't tell you how to handle your shit, but if I was you, which I'm not. I wouldn't sit back and watch the world pass me by."

"What would you do?" Imf asked for his advice.

"I would get it while the getting is good."

"So the getting is good." Imf rubbed his chin.

"Better than ever. The shipment made it through customs. I know the weed and coke won't be a problem for you and your gang. But can you move the heroine?" Panama asked.

"I can handle anything."

"I surely hope so. Now come on, let me show you and Kesha the lovely city."

CHAPTER: Five

"Gurl," Kesha said to Angie and Net as they sat at her house and sipped on Moscato. "I had an amazing time with Imf in Dallas," she smiled, naming things they had done on their trip. "First we went to this five star restaurant with Imf's friend Panama, then we left there and went to a Dallas Cowboy's football game, fuck what you heard, that really is the biggest arena I've ever been in." She told them. "And guess what?"

"What!" They both asked.

"Y'all not gon' believe this," she said, getting up off the couch.

"What?" Angie and Net said in unison.

"Follow me," she told them, heading towards her room to open her closet door.

"Dadadada-damn!" Spat Net, browsing through all the expensive gear in Kesha's closet. "Damn. Who did you rob?" Net asked Kesha.

"Nobody," Kesha smirked. "Imf got them for me," she smiled. "He also got me my favorite, Manolo Blahniks." She hooted and hollered.

Net scanned through a couple of price tags while waiting on Kesha to get done with her charades.

A Gucci dress for two thousand-six-hundred and thirty-dollars, a dress by Burberry of London for eight hundred, a dress by Prada that cost three thousand, and dresses by Fendi and Armani Exchange, oh this tramp gave Imf the ass, she thought, seconds before asking.

"Did you and Imf make out?" She questioned, curiously looking at Kesha.

"No." Kesha answered. "I told you; we just cool like that."

"Bitch! You think I'm that naïve?" Spat Net. "No nigga in his right mind is gonna spend that kinda loot on you and not want something in return. I'm estimating about twenty stacks over here, and you talking about y'all just cool.... Yeah right!"

"Twenty-three, if you include the heels," Kesha stated. "And real talk, nothing happened. Imf just showed me a good time, no correction, the best time," she beamed.

"Let me get this right, you and Imf didn't fuck, and he spent a grip on you."

"Right," she nodded to Net's question. "Not everybody that hangs together has to be together intimately."

"Yeah right, Imf hasn't said it, but he has invested a lot of money in you lately, getting your hair and nails done, taking you on vacations, wining and dining you. I bet he spends more money on you then he does on himself," Net expressed to Kesha as a reminder. "See." Net went on to say. "Imf's on that reverse psychology shit. He knows once you ride first class. There's no way you will ever wanna go back to riding coach." Net used the example of the coach in reference to Silk.

"I don't get it. If Imf was so interested in me. How come he hasn't just come out and said it." Kesha looked at Net, and then Angie with a real puzzled look on her face. Both of them shook their heads in disgust.

"Rejection," stated Net.

"Rejection?" Kesha laughed. "A thug niqqa like Imf?" She questioned.

"Yeah a thug nigga like Imf." Net repeated. "But don't listen to me. Just sit around and give another bitch the opportunity to be where you could've been." Net stated.

* **

"Oh God," Alexis moaned, as Imf pounded her like a Mac truck.

"That's it." She gyrated her hips. She knew what she was doing was wrong, but God it felt so damn good. She held onto Imf's ass as he thrust deep into her, so deep that when he pulled out, there was this smacking sound. "Oh God," she panted, as he plunged back into her.

"I'ma about to bust in this shit," he informed her, balling up into fetal position after his last dash between her thighs.

Alexia cocked her legs wide open, as Imf released his load. She shivered, as he continued to jerk inside her. And with no energy left, she laid back motionless, as she escaped deep in thought. As she rubbed her nipples as Imf pulled out of her to get out of bed. Still feeling sexy, she continued to enjoy her climax. She pressed her finger in and out of wet slit.

"Imf, lick my pussy."

"Suck a dick."

"Stupid nigga."

"Stupid ho."

"I hate you," she lied, as she finger fucked herself.

"Why didn't you use a rubber?" She asked Imf.

"You got me fucked up with your nigga." Imf spat.

"You know I don't wanna get pregnant."

"You should've thought about that before you got here," he lit a blunt and took a puff.

"Come back over here," she toyed with herself. "Let me nut on you."

She hiked her leg up and played in her pussy from the back. Imf moved behind Alexia. Sometimes he couldn't stand her, but he couldn't deny that the bitch had some good pussy. "I'ma squirt all on that dick," she said, as she rode him backwards.

Imf palmed Alexia's ass with one hand, and gripped both of her large double D's with the other. He was so deep in her that he just let her do all the work. He could feel her pulsating her vaginal walls squeezing his manhood tightly.

"I'm coming," Alexia screamed, squirting all over his dick.

He fucked her until he got another nut, then pushed her up off his dick. She damn near went sailing off the bed. She trembled as she tried to gain her composure. Once she got herself together, she curled up under Imf.

"Imf, I want us to be a happy family again."

"Oh, you was happy with me?"

"Yeah, at one point," she admitted.

"Then what changed that?"

"You picked the game over us," she sighed.

"Bitch, I was in the streets when you met me," he barked.

"Yeah, and I thought I could handle that, but I can't." She rubbed his face. "What do you say about us tryna work things out?"

"I think we good as cuddle buddies."

"I'm not your cuddle buddy, I'm your babies momma."

"And shit, I love you for that," he smiled, and then kissed her on her cheek, followed by an affectionate smack on the rear. "You know that's gon' always be my pussy."

"Oh yeah, you know J.T is thinking about putting a ring on it."

"Can that nigga fuck as good as me?"

"No," she smirked. "But dick ain't everything."

"It's important though."

"True!"

"Do you still make him use condoms?"

"Of course I do."

"Then you just wasting your time," he stated, groping his dick. "You suck that nigga off yet?"

"Imf," she uttered.

"Real talk."

"No. You know I don't suck nobody else's dick," she blushed. "Just yours, Big Daddy." She said, easing down to kiss his penis until it was hard.

Then she started deep throating him. She milked him down for nearly twenty minutes before he bust, and dosed off to sleep. Alexia got up and prepared to leave. She needed to go explain to J.T where she had been all night. Yet, she was not worried, she was sure she would figure out something. Before, leaving, she kissed Imf on the cheek and eased out of the hotel room to make her way to her car.

***

Imf had stepped his security up to make sure no problems occurred. Hay-Zeus and Big Timer were out front handling the customers. Tank was handling the surveillance. He had everything from binoculars, walkie talkies, T.V cameras to double pump shot guns, and they were ready for anything. Almost anything.

"Yo Imf, your baby momma here with your son. What you want me to do?" Big Timer chirped over the walkie talkie.

"Send her up," Imf replied, getting off the sofa to walk into the hallway.

Nigga's were shooting a game of dice. He noticed all the niggas in the hallway stopped and stared, forgetting about the dice game when Alexia appeared. Alexia had the resemblance of the actress Anika Rose. She was wearing a loose top and ass hugging coochie cutters.

"This bitch gon' make me kill one of these niggas," Imf uttered to himself.

"Why ain't you happy to see me?" Alexia smirked, as Imf grabbed his son away from her.

"What up, lil Soldier?" He smiled, kissing his little nine month old son.

"Where mines?" Alexia smiled. She placed her hand on her cheek and waited, but a kiss on her cheek never came. Embarrassed, she played it off. "You too gangster to give me a kiss now?"

"What you want?" Imf asked.

"I want us to spend some quality time together, and then maybe later on we can check into the room and spend the night together." Alexia chuckled.

Imf smirked.

"I ain't fucking with you, but we can do the Q.T. thing. Let me go tell Stacks I'm out."

***

They were at Hanes Mall. Alexia had gone on a massive shopping spree, and Imf couldn't wait to get the fuck up out of there..

"Yo. I ain't your nigga."

"Shut up." Alexia spat, flipping through a rack of high priced dresses. "I could look real good in this," she held up a cute dress to show Imf.

"Get that shit and come on." He fussed, holding his son while she shopped.

"I think I'll take this one too," she grabbed another dress without even checking the price. "After we leave here, we'll go to Baby Gap and grab some stuff for your son."

After shopping until she was exhausted, Alexia finally came down on her shopping spree.

"Let me get Mytra and you take the clothes out to the car," she suggested.

"I don't know why you got all this shit anyway," Imf fussed, exchanging their son for six bags of clothes.

"Stop being so cheap. You'll make it back," she responded, making her way to the car.

* * *

I know I said I wasn't fucking with Alexia's dumb ass, but here I was, fucking the shit out of her while my son Mytra was sound asleep, Imf thought, thrusting his dick far into Alexia.

"Deeper." Alexia screamed out.

"Shut the fuck up, you gon' wake my son," Imf glimpsed back, continuing to deep stroke her.

"No we won't," she insisted, cocking her legs wider apart. "Oooo yeah! Right there, Babe! Right there," she encouraged him.

Imf closed his eyes. Shit was feeling so good right now. He could feel her pussy walls clamping against his foreskin. He pulled out and reentered.

"Oh gosh," she sighed and turned sideways. "Slow the fuck down," she groaned in painful pleasure.

Imf burst inside of Alexia and slowly pulled out. Once again, he could hear her pussy making popping sounds. Alexia trembled on the bed and rubbed her erect nipples. Just when Imf thought things were all good. Alexia hit him with some worldwide news.

"Imf," she trembled.

"What?"

"Hold me," she gripped his hand and pulled him to her.

"What's good, Ma?" Imf wrapped his arms around her.

"I want you back in my life."

"What about J.T.?"

"What about him?"

"That nigga care for you."

"But I don't love him the way that I love you," she revealed.

"I don't know what to tell you."

"What in the hell is that suppose to mean?" She sat up.

"It is what it is. You had your chance and you fucked it up."

"What?"

"You chose that square ass nigga over me."

"I'm sorry, Imf. I thought I could change you, but I made a mistake."

"That you did. But yo, I need a ride back to the spot."

"Give me a minute," she snarled at him, and then huffed.

"Okay," Imf walked to the bathroom to wash himself off. Once he started to put his clothes on, Alexia slowly got herself together so she could drive Imf back to the Projects. "Imf please think about it," she asked, gripping his hand.

"Word." Imf kissed his son Mytra on the cheek as he slept in his car seat.

"He looks just like you. Imf. I should have never tried to change you. You're a good man."

"Word," Imf said as he kissed Alexia on the cheek.

As she turned and kissed him on the lips, Imf didn't know this, but Alexia was caught up in a love triangle. She loved J.T. ; however, Imf was fucking her so good, he made her thirst for more. When she drove off, Imf rubbed his chin, thinking to himself, *I gotta put a stop this.*

CHAPTER: Six

Imf was out front in the courtyard when Kesha pulled up.

"Yo. I need you to run me a couple places." He told her.

"I'm running late, Imf. Tell you what, how about I come back through and get you?" Kesha replied.

"Never mind. I'll call a taxi," he told her.

"Get in," Kesha huffed.

"Good looking yo," he said, getting in the car. Imf smiled.

"Umhumm!" She uttered. "Where are we going?"

"I gotta go pick up my son."

"What," she looked at him. "Why didn't you tell me?" She fussed.

"Cause you would've said no," he told her. "Don't worry. I'ma just go in and out."

Kesha was shaking her head at Imf. In the back of her mind she knew Imf made a bad decision by asking her to take him to his B.M's headquarters.

"Right here." Imf pointed.

Kesha pulled over on the side of the road and waited on Imf. At first things seemed alright. But then once his B.M. got a glimpse at her car, all hell broke loose.

"I know you not taking my son around no bitch," she snapped. "Nope! You got me fucked up, I'm not letting my son hang around none of your hood rat bitches," Alexia screamed at Imf.

"Chill out. I thought you wanted to chill with you man," Imf uttered.

"Who is that bitch?" Alexia screamed.

"What's wrong, baby?" J.T asked, walking to the door half undressed. "This niqga bothering you?"

"Butt out nigga," Imf warned.

"Nah, nigga. This my business." J.T folded up his cuffs.

"Yo, I ain't got time for you and your silly ho. Fuck y'all." Imf turned to walk off with his son, when Alexia hopped on his back and bit him.

"Bitch!" He yelled, cringing out in pain.

Imf swung Alexia onto the ground. That's when all hell broke loose. J.T swung, forcing Imf to duck and run.

"Bring your punk ass back," J.T yelled, as Imf ran and hopped into the car. "You alright Lexia?" He held his hand out to help Alexia up.

"No, I'm not alright. I want my damn baby, I don't want my son around that tramp," she fussed, dusting off her backside. "Get my car keys,." she told J.T.

"Where we going?"

"I don't know where you going, but I'm gonna get my son."

* * *

"You know you're bleeding right?" Kesha asked Imf.

"Yeah. That bitch bit the shit out of me."

"That shit was crazy. You may need to go to the hospital," she suggested.

"Nah. Take me to go get a room."

"First I'm gonna get you something to take care of that gash in your back."

***

"It's worse than I thought," Kesha said, as she examined Imf's back.

"Lay down on the bed so I can fix you up." She insisted, easing off the side. "I don't know why you keep fucking with your baby momma. That girl is gonna kill you one day." She laughed.

"Ouch!" He yelped.

"Don't cry now. That's what you get." She teased rubbing his back with peroxide. "I really thought you was smarter than what you are."

"What you mean?" Imf asked, shifting slightly to face her.

"I don't know. It just seems like you wouldn't waste your time with a dingy ass broad like that."

"I know right," Imf smirked.

"When was the last time y'all messed around?"

"What?" He asked, looking back at her. "Yo that shit feels good," he said as she massaged his back.

"Did you fuck her recently?" Kesha quizzed" straddling his back. "I wanna know."

"You really wanna know?" Imf asked.

"Sure do! Or I wouldn't have asked."

"I fucked that bitch last night, and the night before that."

"What!" Kesha smacked him upside his head.

"Ouch." He groaned.

"Stupid." She was so pissed, so she got off his back.

"What I do?" Imf questioned.

"It's what you didn't do," she commented.

"What you mean?"

"You'll figure it out." She replied, sucking her teeth.. "Let me put this band aid on you so I can bounce."

"Bounce then," he replied.

"Imf. Don't do this. You the one who went and did the unthinkable. Why in the hell would you take me over your B.M's crib in the first place. Did you ever stop to think about how she might feel about another woman being around her son?" She crossed her arms together.

"We ain't together."

"But you fucked her last night and the night before that," she fussed.

"It was nothing," he inisted.

"To you, but to her it was everything. You gotta stop playing games," she explained to him. "And kidnapping your son. Why'd you do that?"

"Mines," he uttered.

"Imf. Take him home to his mom. You don't even know the first thing about raising a child." Kesha replied as she took a deep breath.

"So?"

"Imf." She got serious. "Please. For me." She pleaded with him.

"Alright, but fix me up before you be out. This shit hurts," he complained turning his back to her.

"It should hurt." She uttered.

* * *

Imf spent a little quality time with his son. He thought about what Kesha said about him knowing how to raise a baby as he changed his son's pampers, while he fed him and as he walked him around the room in circles, singing nursery rhymes. After about an hour, he called a taxi and headed to his B.M's place. He got out the taxi and went to knock on the door.

Alexia answered the door with an attitude, but was very excited to see her son.

"My baby!" She grabbed Mytra out of Imf's arms. "Where'd you have him? I don't want my baby around no bitches," she elaborated to Imf.

"Yeah, whatever. I could say the same shit about J.T. Where that nigga at?" Imf asked, peering in the door.

"No, Imf," she panicked.

"Just bullshitting," Imf smirked. But tell that nigga the next time he swing on me he got problems."

"Tell that bitch the next time I see her she got problems," Alexia threatened.

"I'm pretty sure she will kick your ass all over the place."

"That's what you think. I'ma drill that bitch if I see her again," Alexia promised.

J.T walked in the living room, drinking a Corona.

"Who is that?" He asked like he didn't know.

"My son's father. He brought Mytra home."

J.T jumped up off the sofa and rushed the door. Alexia saw Imf go into his shirt for his gun.

"Go in the room and wait on me," she said, placing Mytra in J.T's arms before he got himself killed.

"But," he uttered.

"Just do what I asked you," she snapped at him. , After she watched J.T take her son up the steps, she continued. "Can we meet up tonight?" She asked Imf.

"Nah, but nice try. You wanted a square, so you got a square. Enjoy your square ass life and leave me the fuck alone," Imf said before he bounced.

"You alright, baby?" J.T. walked up and kissed Alexia on the back of the neck.

"Leave me alone," she snapped in a rage.

* * *

"Damn, Imf. Slow down," Maliah told him.

"Fuck that!" Imf said, as he devoured her neck with kisses. "All that shit you was telling me you would do when I got back. Twerk something for me," he taunted as he lifted her onto the kitchen sink at her house. "Spread them legs," he ordered, parting her fat thighs.

She moaned as he slid his hand underneath her skirt, and began to finger fuck her.

"Oh," she gasped for air.

"Tell me how you want it." He bent down in a squat position. "You want me to beat it or eat it?" He kissed her thighs with his warm tongue.

"Eat it." She moaned, shifting her body and leaning back.

Imf started eating her coochie through the silky fabric. Slowly, he slid her panties to the side and ate.

"Oh, Imf," Maliah moaned as she gripped his head. "Don't ever stop," ,she said, gasping for air.

"Bet that."

He cocked her legs up and pushed his tongue against her clitoris. Licking her all around, he made her shiver and call out his name. Maliah braced herself so she wouldn't fall into the sink. Imf had her ass cuffed and her legs parted wide. She found herself lying flat back on the kitchen counter in the exact same area she chopped vegetables up and cooked.

"That feels so good. Please don't stop," she begged wiggling her hips.

"Come for me, Ma," he leaned against the counter and licked her sideways, and directly between her thick lips. Then he licked ,in tiny circular motions until she whelp from an orgasm. Imf pulled her off the counter while she was still vibrating. He pulled down his pants and plunged into her from the back.

Maliah held onto the counter as Imf pushed his never ending dick all the way inside her. Then back out and smacked back into her like a Ram.

"Oh Baby."

Imf cocked Maliah's fat rear up in the air to ensure he hit all pussy. He bent her across the counter and long dicked her. With nothing that could be said, he gripped her flapping breast and fucked her fast and hard.

Maliah slowly wiggled against Imf. Her pussy walls grabbed a hold of him, sucking him and making a slurping sound as he pulled out. He was so long and thick that she found herself submitting to him. As he fucked her in all the right places, she cried out.

After a long fuck session, Maliah rubbed Imf's chest. As they laid in her bed naked, she scanned her fingers across Imf's cute face, and toyed with his dreads as he peacefully slept. Kissing him ever so softly, she was tickled as to how intrigued she was with Imf. And because he was a great fuck, she doubted that anyone else could do it as well as he had. He had her speaking in parables, which no one could understand, only a woman getting her fantasy fulfilled.

Imf woke up the next day and Maliah was gone. He got out of bed, and tossed on his gear.

"Maliah!" He called out.

There was a note on the nightstand.

Dear, Imf.

Thanks for last night. It was the bomb! I will be out of town for a few days, so my advice to you, homeboy. Behave until I get back.

P.S. I'm not finished with you yet.
Smiles my way.

A grin flashed across Imf's face as he held the letter in his hand.

"Damn, this girl sure goes out of town a lot," he uttered before he bounced.

* * *

Maliah relaxed on the private jet going to Texas. As she thought of Imf, she smiled. *I'm gonna marry that nigga.* She pondered to herself. *He is the best thing that has happened to me in a long time.* She smiled, thinking about all the bad relationships she had been in. *Let me see ... there was the lawyer that didn't work, umm - conceited bastard. The doctor who was too sophisticated, and then there was Jeff. Damn! He was a real pain in the ass.*

And then there's Imf. Though he is the thug type, which I generally don't tend to go for, him and that good pipe game got me wide open, she grinned. *But he is an avid listener who shows me the upmost attention and affection, and I love that about him.*

"So, who is he?" Beverly, Maliah's long time associate asked.

"You can tell?" Maliah smiled.

"It's written all over your face. Girl, he's got you beaming, and I wanna know who this guy is cause he's also has you wide open."

"Well. His name is Ingram, and he is so amazing! I think I found my soul mate."

* * *

"That nigga ain't shit. Got you selling that bullshit crack," Silk spat. "He whipping that shit up and making a killing off of you." Silk shook his head out of anger. "You gotta be the dumbest broad in the world," he scolded Kesha as she sat on the bed, listening to all the crucial insults Silk hurled at her.

"So, what if he sells me crack. I make good money," she half said.

"You just don't get it, do you? That nigga is using your dumb ass."

"I'm not dumb."

"Then show me." Silk walked out the room and slammed the door.

Kesha got up off the bed, grabbed her purse and keys and drove to Happy Hills to find Imf. She saw Big Timer out front.

"Where is Imf," she asked.

"He's just now rolling up." Big Timer pointed.

Kesha's mouth dropped when she saw Imf kissing a hypnotic girl with a Sun Kiss skin tone. As he hopped out of a black Beamer, she became enraged. So enraged, anger had her fast walking towards the car. She approached him as he stood at the driver side door in a pair of denim jean shorts and wife beater. She folded her arms together while he enjoyed his high class ho.

"Imf, I need to talk to you."

"Cool. Give me a second," he turned and said.

"No. Right now."

"What?" Imf remarked.

"Who is she?" Maliah questioned Imf.

"Bitch, I'm Kesha."

"I got your Bitch Ho! And you don't want none of this." Maliah chuckled.

"Hold up." Imf checked Maliah.

"No, you hold up. I'm out of here," Maliah corrected Imf, pulling off.

"Damn Kesh. That was some dumb shit." Imf got on his cell to call Maliah.

"That bitch got you open." Kesha proclaimed, walking up to Imf. She took his cellular from his hand and shattered it on the ground. "That's how I feel about that ho." Kesha snapped.

Everyone and they momma was out and about on this particular day. Imf had to be cool. For one, Kesha was his road dawg, so he would never allow himself to spass out on her, which is why he paused to inhale and exhale.

"Fuck the phone. What you wanna talk about?"

"Don't try and play me Imf." She pointed her finger in his face.

"Whoa!" Imf turned his head to the side, and even still Kesha was going berserk shouting at him.

"I should've known that your ass wasn't shit. You been playing me for a fool all this time." She pressed Imf's face with the back of her hand, showing major signs of disrespect.

"Fuck you. I thought you was different," she sassed, walking off.

Imf could've stopped her, but he didn't. His reaction was so much different from others. While people laughed. He was tryna figure out what the fuck Kesha had spassed out on him for.

***

No lie. Seeing Imf with that bitch had me about to have a nervous breakdown. I declared to myself that I would've shot that raggedy heffah had she not pulled off, Kesha was bobbling with her thoughts when her cell rung. She wiped the tears that had formed in her eyes.

"What!" She answered.

"What's wrong with you?" Net asked.

"Nothing, I don't feel like talking." She said immediately ending the call.

Her cell began ringing again. She knew it was just Net calling back to see if she was alright. She ignored it. When it kept ringing, irritating the hell out of her. She answered,

"Hello."

"Yo, tell me you PMSing." Imf asked.

"Fuck you, Imf."

"Nah, fuck wit' me." He got out before she hung up.

After her last call from Imf's, Kesha screened the rest of her incoming calls.

"What!" She answered.

"So, you beefin' wit' me now and shit!"

"Imf, I'm not in the mood for this right now."

"When you gon' be in the mood?"

"Never."

"So," he paused. "It's like that?"

"Yeah, exactly like that. I'll bring that money I owe you. I think it's best that we both go our separate ways."

"Some things ain't always about money. Keep that shit," he hung up.

Kesha was silent. She couldn't believe Imf had just hung up on her.

After all the shit we've been through, she pondered as Silk walked in the house. He didn't even speak; he just went into the kitchen. She waited a few minutes and followed.

"Silk." She called out.

Silk was mixing coke into rock form.

"What."

"What are you doing?"

"What it look like," he shot back, continuing to do wonders with the coke.

"Silk. I wanna learn how to cook, will you teach me?"

"Nah, why would I teach you how to cook when you flipping another nigga's coke." He snarled, giving her a convicting look.

"Dumb bitch," he said out loud. "I can see if you was on my team or whatever."

"So, what if I decide to get down with the team?"

"Then that's a whole nother story." It's about damn time." He did some wishful thinking. "You see those two ounces on the table right there?" She nodded. "Yeah, flip those for me and I might think about it." He said to her as he shifted and stirred the coke.

"How much you want me to bring you back?" Kesha asked, picking up the two ounces from the table.

"Since it's you, just bring me back nineteen hundred."

"That's kind of steep." She told Silk.

Especially when Imf was selling her ounces for seven fifty sometimes seven twenty five or seven hundred.

"Yo. Maybe when you flip a few more ounces for me, the price will go down. Until then, help me get to the top."

"And when you reach the top, you gon' take me with you?" She remarked.

"Ain't no secret. Let's get this money like I know you can."

* * *

It felt good being at the top. Also, knowing no one could fuck wit' you was a bonus too. Imf and his crew had the exotic weed on lock, ecstasy, H-which most knew as Heroin, plus the crack game on smash.

Imf called up Maliah. She wasn't answering. When she did answer, he could tell she was still tripping off of Kesha.

"Yo," he said.

"What?"

"You finally decided to answer the damn phone?"

"Started not too," she retorted.

"Then why you answer?"

"I don't know."

"I'm on my way over." He hung up. "Yo Tank. Let me borrow your keys" Tank tossed Imf the keys to his Lincoln Navigator. "Be back later. Don't get sloppy." He told everyone.

"Nigga. We never do." Tank expressed, flipping out his cell to call Big Timer to let him know that Imf was coming down.

Imf got downstairs and saw Big Timer talking to some girl with a cute face and round ass.

"I see you stay busy."

"All the time." Big Timer shot back.

Imf hopped in to the Large SUV and drove off. He drove to Maliah's house in Clemons. He got out the SUV and made his way to her door. He knocked a few times, but she didn't answer, so he became impatient and called her phone.

"What!" She answered.

"Open the door. You know I'm out here," he hung up.

Seconds later, Maliah opened the door. Instead of inviting him in, she left it slightly ajar and took a seat on the couch with her palm on her cheek. Leaning against the arm rest, she pouted as Imf entered.

"Yo," Imf tapped her arm.

"Get off me," she snapped, snatching her arm away from him.

"Why you ain't called me in a week?" He asked, gripping his belt buckle.

"Cause I didn't wanna see you."

"What about now?" He gripped his private.

"I hate you."

"You mean that? I had something for you too," he nudged her head. "Now you can't get it."

"Imf," she stood up. "Let me see it."

"Nah, you ain't been acting right," he teased, flopping on the couch.

She sat back down beside him, and wrapped her arm around him.

"What you got for me?"

"Nah, fuck it. You blew it."

"Imf, come on. I want it."

"How bad?"

"Just give it to me," she rubbed his stout chest.

"I don't think you ready."

"I'm ready." She kissed him.

"You sure?" He asked, as she tugged on his bottom lip with her teeth.

"Yeah I'm sure," she replied, straddling his lap to lock lips with him.

"Close your eyes," he smiled. "Gosh you are so beautiful." He said.

"Thanks," she smiled with her eyes shut. "Now lift up."

"What."

"Lift up."

She leaned forward.

Imf pulled his shorts down. "Okay. Sit back down," he told her. "You like what I got for you?" he asked as she giggled and kissed him.

"Yes, of course."

"Then show me."

"What you want, bay?"

"Bless me," he smirked.

"Oh, you must mean some head. Does what's her name suck your dick?" She asked. Maliah bent down in a squatting position. "Is she better than me?"

"Damn." Imf moaned as she took him in her mouth.

"Is she?" Maliah looked up at him.

Imf didn't say shit. Maliah was the next super head, and got mad when he didn't answer. She began bobbing up and down frantically. Then she started deep throating him relentlessly. Maliah sucked the tip of his thick erection and licked him down to the bone. She moaned and groaned as he slid her Teddy to the side and played in her pussy while she sucked his dick.

"Cock that thang up," Imf said, raising his hand to smack her ass. He eased back on the sofa, and she did what he asked in one swift motion. He immediately pulled her down across his face in the 69 position, causing shit to get real intense as they pleasured each other.

Imf busted and Maliah moved away from his hard climax. She positioned herself on the arm of the chair, reached back and pulled Imf towards her.

"Fuck me like you fuck that little black bitch." She talked reckless to Imf. "I bet she can't give head better than me, can she?" She looked back at Imf as he entered her.

Imf didn't reply. He snatched Maliah back against his dick real hard, ramming her wet pussy with force.

"Oww!" She cringed. "I know her pussy ain't as deep as mine. Wetter than mine," Maliah spat. "I don't know what you see in her besides an okay body... Awh! A plain face ...Awh! That... That bitch is busted." She gasped gripping the cushions on the sofa as Imf continued to rammed into her. "Is this how you fuck that dirty ho too?" Maliah stirred her ass up. "And my ass is bigger than hers as well."

Imf tossed Maliah onto her back and shut her up by slopping her down with a wet kiss. As he moved up and down, the tip of his erection curled up into her G-spot. Maliah gripped the crevice of Imf's ass, as he fucked her in the Cat position. He slightly towered over her, pressing against her top most sensitive spot. This was also the spot that was the easiest to make a woman go to that special place called orgasm, which was confirmed as she spread her legs wider as he went deeper and deeper.

"Damn, Imf. I don't want you to stop." Maliah whispered as she gyrated her hips.

"You love me?" He asked, pulling out and sliding back inside her.

"Yeah, Imf."

"Tell me."

"I do Imf." Was all she could say before she shook from multiple orgasms.

"You alright," Imf asked, flopping on the sofa beside Maliah.

She didn't respond. She was still vibrating from her climax. After a minute or two, she got herself back together.

"Imf, baby. I really do love you with all that I am."

"You really mean that?"

"I do," she said kissing Imf.

***

"Yo, Imf. You got one hell of a girl." Stack's said as Maliah pulled up at the Waffle House. "How come don't nobody know that bitch."

"I guess she stay low key." Imf replied.

"She ain't that low key. Don't nobody at the strip club know that bitch." Stack's said as he watched Maliah get out the car and walk towards Imf.

"Sup, Ma?" Imf kissed Maliah.

"Yo. You still work at Daddio's?" Stacks' questioned.

"Cause I checked around. Funny, how nobody knows you."

"I only danced there one time." She clung onto Imf's arm.

"So, where you work at now?" Stack's continued.

"That's enough." Imf interfered.

"This bitch ain't no good. You better watch her," Stacks' scolded. "I know a snake when I see one." He warned. "You fuck up mines, I'm coming to see you." Stacks' swore.

"What are you insinuating?" She stood her ground.

"Check this bitch for a wire," Stack's said.

"Hold up." Imf calmed his clique down.

"You just wanna have a reason to see me naked, you pervert," Maliah spat.

"She got you on that one," Tank laughed, along with their whole damn clique.

Imf pulled Maliah up to him and started caressing the small of her back to the fat crease in her ass.

"You got on a wire?" He slobbed her down with a kiss in front of his crew.

"Lift up my dress to see," she teased as Imf stroked her large ass in front of his friends.

"Yeah, Imf," Big Timer replied.

"Yeah. She might be wearing a wire," Tank said.

"Lift up that dress. You never can tell these days," Hay-Zeus said.

"Your boys want a free peep show," Maliah said as she grinned at Imf.

"Should I give them one?" He asked as he rubbed her round ass.

"That's up to you," She told Imf.

Imf kissed Maliah, and then lifted her tight mini dress that hugged her curves, for all to see.

"Yo. Is she wired?" Imf asked his crew.

"She wired alright," Hay-Zeus responded, covering his mouth with the palm of his hand.

"Yo," Imf smirked. "Next time I'ma have to charge y'all niggas." Imf said. "But yo." He pounded everyone up. "Me and the lady gotta be out. We 'bout to get it in, if you know what I mean." He winked at Stacks.

"I'm watching you Bitch." Stacks' mouthed, so the only one who could make out his words was Maliah.

"Yo. I'm sorry about that back there," Imf said, getting into Maliah's black Beamer.

"Got me showing my ass in front of everyone and shit," She teased.

"Yo. I hope you understand that they just worry about me," Imf laughed and explained.

"They should," she scanned his jawbone with her hand. "They love you, but I love you more," she acknowledged. "And I would never do anything to hurt you."

Maliah stood by the window looking out as the wind blew freely. She was between a rock and a hard place. Here she was involved with someone who was so good to her, but on the other hand, so harmful to others. She glanced back at Imf as he slept. She wanted to share her world with him and give him all that he desired. But in order to do that, she had to get him to ease out of the dope game. Feeling sexy, she made her way over to the bed.

"Imf," she called his name, straddling him.

"What?"

"If I asked you to, would you leave the game?" She questioned him, as she started riding him.

"What kind of shit is that?" He looked up at her perky breast.

"I like when you look at me like that." She squeezed both breast with her hands.

"I like the way you make me feel like I'm the only one that matters. Let me help make your life a better world." She began to ride him with a passion and fire that she began to think that Imf would leave the game for her. "Let's get married. Have kids of our own. A girl for me. A boy for you. I want you to give me your child." She pressed down on his chest with both hands and positioned herself in the reverse cowgirl position.

Imf's face started twitching. He was in a submission hold. He couldn't do shit but be entertained by the things Maliah was showing him. She took him to new heights. And word, he loved the shit out of her mouth. He didn't say one single word. Probably because he didn't wanna rain on her parade.

"Fuck me. Imf. Let's move somewhere and start a family together. I can take care of you. You don't have to do shit!!" She bit down on her bottom lip. "I'll take care of you." She rubbed her erect nipples. "Say something. Talk to me."

"Word. Damn. Um. God. Jesus," he said as he released inside her.

Maliah locked her body around Imf and took in his load. Wanting to have his child, she rode him until he was through making love to her. Once done, she slid from his huge dick and collapsed on the bed. As her legs trembled, her body rumbled from the rapture of love.

"Imf," she said.

"Yo," he responded, spaced the fuck out and looking up at the ceiling.

"I love you," she uttered. "Please seriously think about what I talked to you about."

"I already did," he griped his crotch.

"What did you decide?" She asked.

"I ain't leaving the game, but we can still kick it."

"What!" She snapped at him. "Imf, I'm telling you I can't be with you if you out here in these streets."

"Bitch! When you met me I was in these streets. Why the sudden change now?"

She took a deep sigh. "Imf. Excuse me if I want what's best for you. Hustling is not a long time career."

"And neither is dancing. I didn't say shit about that."

"Imf. Dancing is not gonna get anyone killed."

"What about Aids?"

"Harder catching that then a freakin' bullet." She said nonchalantly.

"See. That's why I love you," Imf busted out in laughter.

"You should," she swallowed. "Imf, I'm only looking out for your own good."

"Well thanks Ma. Now can we get back to making these kids you keep talking about?" He teased, grabbing her behind.

"No doubt."

CHAPTER: Seven

"Yo. Ain't that Imf and them going to V.I.P." Net said to Angie.

"You know it is," Angie snapped her finger. "Let's go see if he can get us in V.I.P." She said as she and Net made their way over to V.I.P.

"Yo. Hold it. Where y'all think y'all going?" The bouncer stuck his arm out.

"You better get your hand off me. I'm telling you. Trust me, you don't want no problems." Net snapped.

"Is that right?" The bouncer sort of laughed. "Can y'all step back? This is V.I.P." He looked at their Kool-Aid colored hair and joked. "This is not the audition for the Nikki Minaja video," he laughed at his own joke.

"Fucker!" Angle snapped.

"Yo. Angie. Net," Imf said as he walked up.

"Hey, Imf." The bouncer greeted him.

"What up? My gang in there?" Imf asked.

"Yeah. Stacks, Hay-Zeus, Big Timer, and Tank." He named everyone.

"Good. Y'all coming in?" He looked at Angie and Net as they both laughed.

"No doubt, Big Bro," Net smirked and stuck her tongue out at the bouncer.

"I didn't know he was your brother," the bouncer replied.

"Yeah, and I bet he wouldn't like your little joke either." Net glared at the bouncer.

"What joke?" Imf placed his arms around both ladies.

"Wasn't that funny," Net replied, rolling her eyes at the bouncer as they rolled in V.I.P.

They took a seat and Imf started ordering them the drinks of their choice. Net and Angie scrunched up against Imf at the table. Everyone was tipsy and having a good time. Net enjoyed Imf's company the most, but the truth of the matter was, she knew Imf would never take her serious if she told him she was feeling him; especially since he kept wanting insight on Kesha. She took that as a sign.

"You know Imf. I'm pretty sure she'd be happy to hear from you. All you had to do was ask me for her number." She grabbed his Black Berry and stored Kesha's info in it.

"What up with your cousin Stacks?" She hinted, searching the room for his fine ass.

"Stacks," Imf called, motioning for him to come over. "Yo. This my little sis, so take care of her my nigga. Now I'm about to break out," he dapped Stacks' up.

"Yo. What up, Angie?" He said, looking back as he felt someone tugging at his shirt.

"What's up with him?" She wanted to know, pointing at Big Tank.

"I don't know," Imf responded as he called Big Tank over.

He didn't think Angie was his type, but the nigga had one too many drinks, so anything was possible. He acquainted the two before he bounced with Hay-Zeus, who was driving his new Denali Truck.

"Look at them punk mu'fuckers," Silk said as him and his manz Chocolate Tie sat in his Range Rover. "Yo, I want you to rob that nigga and anybody else with him. That nigga is easy to get. Follow that nigga and get back with me when it's about that time."

"Word." Chocolate Tie said as he blew out dark clouds of smoke.

He knew this would be his toughest assignment yet. He could for one, tell Silk that this job was impossible and back out of it like a little scared bitch. Or two, take the assignment and become a thousandnaire. Of course, the thought of getting money it is a given that the assignment is a no brainer.

"I'll take it."

"Good," Silk went in his pocket and pulled out five grand. "I want that nigga's head on a platter."

"This all of it?" Chocolate Tie asked, sticking the manila envelope in his shirt pocket.

"Hell no! Half now and half later." Silk insisted.

Chocolate Tie's name was ringing bells on the street. He was one of the most rugged stickup kids - murderers in the notorious Rollin Hills area. So with that in mind, Silk felt good about his hired gun.

CHAPTER: Eight

Kesha rolled up to one of her client's trap spots. She got out the car and made her way inside. An old lady by the name of Rose answered the door to let her in.

"Hey Rose." She smiled.

She loved Rose. Rose was some of her reasons for success. On a good day, she could make anywhere from a grand to five thousand just by sitting at Rose's house. Rose did get high, but she was all about the money, so Kesha could leave her little pack's and not have to worry about getting ripped.

"You got that money?" She asked Rose.

"Yeah, I got it." Rose dug in her bra and pulled out a wad of cash. Her face was somewhat sad.

"What's up?" Kesha asked. "Didn't you make any money?" She questioned, sensing something was wrong from Rose's distorted face.

"I hope you ain't got the same thing. I had problems selling it," she told Kesha.

"Oh." Kesha let out a worried sigh. "Look Rose, I need your help to help me get rid of this. I promise when I get my next batch I will look out for you."

"I know you will girl," Rose replied. "Give me what you want me to sell for you, and I'll see if I can get rid of it." She held her hand out.

"I love you so much," Kesha kissed Rose's cheek.

"You better," she rolled her eyes and placed her hands on her stout hips. "Whoever you dealing with, you need to cut them off." Rose gave Kesha some friendly advice.

"I will, momma," she said, waving goodbye.

Kesha went to Unique's trap spot, who was another one of her clients. He's a young hustler and one of her best and most reliable workers. After Kesha pulled up in front of his house, she got out her car.

"Yo, you got that money?"

"Yeah, but I'm a little short this time." Unique placed the money in her hand. "That's eighteen hundred."

"Unique." She whined. "You know I don't take shorts." She let out a deep sigh.

"I know, I know, but yo that shit's hard as hell to get off. It's mostly water and the customer's don't really like it. I wouldn't lie to you."

"I know Unique." She took a deep sigh. "You always keep it real with me. How about you let me get the two hundred you owe me, that way I can pay my people and get some better work."

"Word." Unique answered, digging in his pocket to pull out the last little bit of money that he was about to flip to get Kesha's money and gave it to her.

It had been a very long and exhausting day for Kesha. She drove to Dutch Village where Net stayed. As she pulled up and watched Stacks and Big Tank leaving Net's apartment, she waved.

"Hey y'all." She flagged Tank and Stacks down. "What y'all doing over here?" She questioned them as they climbed into Stacks' SUV.

"Damn you nosey. Find something to do with yourself Little Momma," Stacks said, backing out from in front of Net's crib and pulled off.

Kesha beat on Net's door. "Open up," she banged.

"What?" Angie snatched the door open.

"Somebody better tell me why I saw Stacks and Tank walking out of here." Kesha questioned.

"You would know if your bourgeois ass would get out the house some. Well. Anyway." Angie went on rambling. "We went to the Fu-Bar last night and we saw your man Imf, and he was looking better than ever. He kept asking about you, so Net gave him your number."

"She did what?" Kesha complained.

"Girl! You can't stay mad at that nigga about no bullshit. He's only human," Angie told Kesha.

As soon as she said those words, Kesha's cellular went off.

"Hello," Kesha answered.

"Hey you."

"Hey, Imf." Kasha replied as a smile came across her entire face.

"Hey, Bro!" Angie yelled into the phone. "My girl said she loves you, so stop playing games and make it official."

"Move," Kesha playfully shoved Angie in the back. "Sorry about her," Kesha said. "That girl's crazy." She shifted her eyes at Angie for putting her on blast.

"What do I owe to the pleasure of this call?" She sat down on the couch to talk as Angie ear hustled.

"Just checking to see how my friend's doing. That's it."

"Oh. That's it?" She smacked her lips. "I guess I'm doing alright.

"See there you go."

"What."

"That guessing shit!"

"Well," she giggled a little.

"How come you ain't been checking a nigga. I wish you was still over here holding me down."

"I tried that and it didn't work, remember."

"Why not?"

"Don't even go there," she bluntly told him.

"I got time. I'm listening."

"Now you got time, right? You ain't have too much time when your little friend was around." She tossed that in his face as a reminder. "You ignored me for some off brand bitch," she checked Imf. "You just don't know how mad I was at you," she vented.

"Broke my phone."

"I should've," she replied. "And tell your girlfriend whoever she is, I owe her an ass whooping."

"Don't tell me you jealous?" He smirked.

"I might be," she admitted. "Can I confess something to you?"

"It's your world. I'm just in it," Imf stated.

"Well, I guess I was a little jealous. I always thought we had a little chemistry," she admitted.

"We do, but then theirs Silk."

"And that girl you was with," she quickly stated. "How serious are y'all?"

"Can't really tell right now."

"So y'all fucking."

"What kind of shit is that?" He asked Kesha.

"Well?" She asked, waiting patiently for an answer.

"You ain't gon' tell me?"

"That ain't none of your business," Imf told her.

"Ain't none of my business," she repeated. "Why can't you be a man and just tell me the truth?" She asked Imf.

"Cause that shit ain't got nothing to do with why I haven't seen you in almost a month."

"Do you wanna see me, Imf?"

"What you think?"

"Answer."

"Yeah."

"So say it."

He laughed, but didn't answer.

"Your girls tell you we hung out last night?"

"Yeah, they did, now give me an answer Imf!"

"You know I do. You my main squeeze," he answered.

"Well I can't tell."

"Cause you ain't let me squeeze you yet."

"You wanna squeeze me?" She teased. "Cause I wanna squeeze you."

"Kesh. You know I don't play no games."

"Who said I was playing," she laughed.

"Four Seasons Hotel in Greensboro tonight at about nine. I'll call you back and hit you up with the info," he told her.

"Alright," she said. "Don't play no games."

"I never do," she shoved Angie away from the phone. "See you then," she smiled, hanging up.

"It's going down." Angie laughed.

"And you know it," Kasha replied. "I gotta go and get my hair and nails done so I can get on point."

"Imf gon' fuck the shit out of you," Angie joked.

"Shut up." Kesha shoved her. "You coming with me?" She asked.

"Yeah. Let me wake Net up," Angie replied. "No. Let her sleep. I'm pretty sure she must be tired cause I hate to say it, but Stacks' ass is a little pervert."

* *

"My nigga," Stacks bragged. "I tore that pussy up. She flexible too, I had her ass in the power driver."

"What the fuck is that?" Hay-Zeus chuckled. "When you fold a bitch up like this," Stacks demonstrated. "And just fuck her like this." He started humping the air. "Piped Shorty down four times in one night, and then once this morning," he boasted.

"That pussy must be like that?" Hay-Zeus asked Stacks.

"Like eating a Peppermint Patty," Stacks' stated.

"You nasty mu'fucker," Hay-Zeus shoved Stacks. "You done went and ate that bitch's pussy."

"See, you laughing, but if you plan on keeping a bitch you better eat a bitch," he kidded.

"Nah, see I just beat a bitch," Big Tank dry humped the air.

"Oh shit. I know you aint fuck Big Angie," Stacks' covered his mouth in amazement.

"Word." Tank laughed, still stroking the air as he moved his hand like he was smacking her rear end.

"You fucked Pancake Butt," Hay-Zeus teased Tank.

"Yeah. Like this." Tank showed them. "I moved that thong to the side," he said, ramming the air.

"This nigga's a mad man," Stacks' bugged out.

"What did you expect? Shit! You can't be the only one getting his swerve on," Tank dapped Hay-Zeus up. "But yo, y'all sleeping on Angie." *That bitch got some good pussy and some bomb head,* he thought about Angie. "Pancakes or not, I'ma hit Shorty up pretty soon. She said she could get me a hook up on some clothes." He fixed his Polo shirt. "Tank ain't turning down nothing but his collar."

Everyone laughed. Then something came to Stacks' attention.

"Yo, where Trick been?" It's almost like he vanished off the face of the earth.

"I don't know. I ain't seen that mu'fucker," Hay-Zeus replied.

As soon as those words came out of his mouth. The door caved in and shots rang out. Hay-Zeus dove on the floor and started busting his 45. to stay alive. Big Tank and Stack's did the same. Whoever it was trying to kill them was sloppy as hell. Stupid mu'fuckers were shooting up high with an assault rifle like they were killing something, but were really wasting shells. Suddenly, the one with the rifle stopped firing.

"I'm out of shells," he yelled, looking towards his three partners.

"Don't worry about it,." Stack came up from behind the couch and started blasting his double barrel shot gun. "Take that!" he yelled, spraying one of the guys. The other three got ghost. "Don't run now!" Stacks shouted, chasing them down to blast on them. Whoever they were, they ended up getting away.

Big Tank ripped the mask off the cock sucker who had just tried to rob him. He quickly stuck his 44 Magnum in the assailants mouth.

"Suck on these," he stated about to blow his head off. Out of nowhere, Stacks stopped him.

"Hold up," Stack's calmed Tank. "This nigga's young. Who sent you?" "Yo, I know this little nigga," Stack's remembered. "Little Shorty, I used to send you to go get blunts at the candy lady house. Nigga, who sent yo' little ass?" Stacks smashed his Jordan against his head. "And you better start talking." He angrily snapped, putting his foot prints in little manz skull.

"I can't tell you," he moaned and coughed up blood.

"You can, if you wanna live." Stacks continued to put a major stump down on the youngster. He talked to him and whipped his ass at the same time. "Who, mu'fuckin' sent you? Who! Sent! You!" He jumped up as high as he could and leap on his rib cage.

"Ahh!" The young kid shouted. "You tryna kill me." He clutched his side, hanging onto his large intestines. Stacks was about to jump again and was sure to break this mu'fuckers rib cage and sternum. He stopped him in the process.

"Okay." He pleaded. "I'll tell you!"

"I'm listening," Stacks said, pressing his foot down on his chest.

"Trick!" He screamed. "Don't kill me!" He pled.

"I'm not," Stack's answered. "But he is," he motioned to Tank who immediately pulled the trigger. "Boom."

"Now that's what I call a closed casket," Hay-Zeus stated as he turned to look away from the horrible scene.

"Come on. Let's get out of here before the police come. Call Imf," he told Hay-Zeus.

* * *

Imf's phone was turned off. He and Kesha were too busy listening to R. Kelly's slow jam, *Seems Like Your Ready.*

Kesha kissed Imf slowly from his kissable lips all the way down to his muscled bound chest. Kesha was panting. Her vagina was throbbing with every kiss she applied on Imf's neck.

"I want you," she whispered in his ear.

"You got me," Imf replied. After kissing her, he sat back on the bed.

As they spent time at Four Seasons, they drunk a little Hennessy and smoked a little Purple Haze.

"I wanna see what you look like outta them clothes."

"You do?" She asked, kissing him.

"Fo' sho."

Kesha reached over and hit the switch on the lamp. Imf turned the lamp back on.

"Imf." She said in the process of taking off her top.

"I thought you was ready?"

"I am," she replied.

"Then what you waiting for. Hurry up and get out of them clothes."

"I don't like my body," she huffed and mumbled a few words.

"Why not?" Imf looked at her with amazement.

"Cause I'm too fat," she said with a look of discontent.

"Who told you that?"

"Silk," she responded and looked away.

"Fuck him. Lay back while I get undressed," he told her. *That nigga Silk don't know any better or else he would do better,* Imf thought to himself, as he came out of his pants.

Kesha looked at Imf wide eyed. She wasn't gonna tell him that he was stout, but she was thinking just that to herself.

"That nigga don't deserve you, and he can't do you like I can do you." Imf squatted between Kesha's legs and took her in his mouth.

Kesha arched her back.

"You like that?" She asked as she rubbed his dreads. "How does it taste?"

"Good," he replied.

"Ow," she moaned.

Imf parted her lips and licked circles around her clitoris until she started gyrating her hips and thrusting her pubic hair against his slithering tongue. Imf pushed his tongue deep against her clit. At that point, he went down and swiped her sideways from her G-spot to her ass crack. Kesha turned over and let him lick her from the back. Imf inserted his finger and she moaned and backed up against him. Rubbing up against anything she could come across, Imf placed his face between her ass cheeks and tossed her salad.

"Oh God!" Kesha shouted.

"Damn, this shits wet." He licked her from the front of her pussy to the back, then to her asshole.

Kesha couldn't control the climax that was building inside of her. She started thrusting up against his face.

"I'm cumming," she shook.

"Damn," Imf wiped his face as Kesha's juices squirted all over him, and then she collapsed against the bed.

"I'm sorry, I didn't mean too." She said totally embarrassed. "That's never happened to me before."

"I didn't know you was a squirter," he smirked as he flipped Kesha over and climbed on top of her.

"Me neither," she rocked her hips with his, matching his tempo.

"Do that shit again." He told her. "Cum for me, and be yourself." He encouraged her.

Kesha rotated her hips and wrapped her legs around Imf's butt cheeks.

"Cum for me, Daddy." She seduced. "Tell me I'm the one," she said, kissing him. As he plowed into her, she kissed him more passionately.

"You the one," Imf repeated and closed his eyes.

"Cum for me," she said, wrapping her arms around his neck. "Fuck me, Imf. Fuck me hard."

Imf lunged into Kesha until he was rock bottom.

"Like that?" He asked before he sucked on her neck.

"Um-hum." She bit down on her bottom lip.

Imf started moving faster, more aggressive, more tense, fucking her to the point of no return. She moaned and turned her head to the side as his dreads beat up against her face. She curled her legs around his backside.

"I'm about to buss," Imf called out as he plowed down into Kesha.

"Don't pull out," she whispered, locking her legs around him.

"Got-damn." He moaned as he shot his load into Kesha. "Damn, Kesh."

"What?" She smirked as she rocked her hips into him at a slow groove. "Let's hit the shower before I have to get up out of here."

"Can't you stay with me tonight?" Imf asked as he kissed her.

"Can't. Have to go home." Kesha kissed him back.

"To be with him, right?" Imf rolled up off of Kesha.

"Imf. Don't do this," she told him. "You know what time it is?" She kissed on his chest.

"Move. Kesh," he said agitated.

"You move me." She straddled herself on top of him. "You mad?" She asked, kissing him. "If you're mad then do something about it," she inserted him into her slit. Imf was still kinda limp, but he wanted to show this bitch Kesha who she was dealing with. He griped her round ass and Kesha leaned back and started the process of getting Imf back up.

"Don't tell me you can't get it back up. What? You only good for one round?" She smirked. "That's it." She bit down on her bottom lip as he began to come alive.

"This is my pussy," Imf said. Then leaned up and started licking her C-Cups and sucking her perky nipples like grapes.

"Ahh!" She cringed. "Stop!" She smacked his cheek. "What are you tryna do?"

"Put Imf on you," he kept sucking her tits for the hell of it. Just so Silk could see.

"You ain't right." She told him.

"And you are?" He responded as he started banging her pussy out like there was no tomorrow.

Kesha's breast swayed every which way as she gave it to Imf like he was giving it to her. She fucked him real good and vise versa. The next morning, Kesha woke up with a banging headache and as naked as the day she was born.

"Oh shit," she panicked. Why didn't you wake me up?" She asked Imf as he sat on the ledge of the window, puffing on a fat blunt.

"You was sleeping."

"You did this on purpose," she snarled.

"Damn," he laughed. I don't know what you so in a rush to go home for. That nigga gon' kill you fo' sho when he see that." He looked, pointing down at her flesh.

"Oh God!" She sighed, seeing passion marks everywhere.

"Yeah." Imf laughed. I fucked and sucked you real good last night."

"Stupid ass!" She fussed and stormed to the shower.

Imf joined her in the shower and fucked her one more time before she left.

***

Good thing Silk wasn't home when I got here, thought Kesha as she tip toed into the house. Imf had fucked and sucked her so good, it was beyond crazy. That freaky ass nigga had left hickeys from her neck and breast down to her pussy and thighs. Real talk, she was gone off of Imf's love making. She flopped on the couch and dialed up Net's number.

"Yo, girl. That nigga fucked me like it was no one's business. Ate my pussy like Jello and sucked my breast like grapes. I must've fucked him until he passed out," she lied, knowing it was really the other way around.

"How was his stamina?" Net asked.

"He was okay."

She wasn't tryna give Net all the T.M.I. because she knew that in this day and age, anything you told your friend could come back and haunt you. She knew better than to tell it all. Some things had to be kept on the low.

"Silk is gonna kill me once he see's all of these damn passion marks."

"How are you gonna hide them. I heard you can use make up," Net gave her some helpful advice.

"That I just might do. I'll think of something," she told Net.

Imf pulled up in front of the projects in a yellow taxi. It wasn't until he got in front of his project that he saw police everywhere. I'm talking damn near the hold Winston Salem Police Force.

What the fuck happened, he asked himself as he paid the taxi and hopped out.

"Don't go up there, Imf." A bug eyed crackhead told him. "Some young kid got killed last night. Got the police chief and the Channel 8 News all around this bitch."

"I'm here in Happy Hill Gardens, live and direct. From my understanding, a sixteen year old kid was found dead in what is now being described as a wrongful death case. Police would like anyone with information to please contact the number on the screen." The news anchor said. "Reporting to you live and direct, this is Sandra Harding."

"Cut," the camera man said.

"Oh shit," was all Imf could say. He got on his cell and called Stacks.

"Yo." Stacks pick up.

"Shit's crazy." Imf emphasized. "Police e'rerywhere. Even the Chief of Police. And hold up," Imf said as he noticed a school bus full of conscious protesters screaming, "No justice, no peace."

People were riled up about the murder of a minor.

"This is a damn shame," Imf stressed. A nigga couldn't even get a shot of pussy these days without something going awfully wrong. "What happened?" He inquired.

"Nigga's rushed in on us and we had to pop one of their tops. Ain't no more?" Stack's gave him a short briefing.

"So y'all didn't think to move the body, stupid?" Imf blasted. "I knew you wasn't capable of holding shit down."

"Hold up. Where were you when niggas were in combat about to get they freaking wigs split?" Stacks' blurred out, making a valid point.

"Fuck it. You better hope shit play out right. Where y'all at?"

"We somewhere real low. If I was you, I would do the same," Stacks told him.

"Word. Hold up, Taxi," Imf said before the driver pulled off.

Since Imf didn't have a crib with a spare key, he hitched a ride to his safe haven, which was Maliah's crib.

* * *

"Back the fuck up," Maliah shoved Jeff away. She placed her finger directly in his face and told him, "Don't you ever touch me as long as live."

"Somebody's awfully pushy today. I just thought we could get together like old times," Jeff snickered.

She hated him. Her and Jeff had been having an intimate relationship off and on ,but more off than on.

"You know you love me baby." He continued to snicker.

"How can you think it was more than casual sex if anything?" She frowned as she glared at him, totally hating what stood before her.

"Cause the way you screamed my name."

He placed his hands behind his head and thrust his hips like the wrestler, "Ravishing" Rich Rude, as he does his I fucked you dance.

"Asshole," she snarled, shoving past him.

"I'm watching you," he shouted after she walked off.

Maliah was dead tired after a long flight from Texas. She had gotten home and heard loud music. She smiled, because she realized her baby was over.

"Imf!" she called out.

"What, Baby?" He stepped out of the kitchen, sipping on a Heineken. He looked down at her bags. "Where you been?"

"I had to go out of town for a few days." She told him.

"Four to be exact," he announced, rocking to the music. "You want me to take your luggage upstairs.

"Can you Baby?" She handed over her suitcase and tote bag. "Thanks," she said, smiling.

"No problem," he carried her bags upstairs. Curiosity got the best of him. He began to check Maliah's bags while she was in the kitchen. Nothing out of the ordinary, but he still had questions. "Yo, Maliah," he called out as he heard her in the kitchen.

"Yeah."

"Bring your ass up here."

"What, Imf?" Maliah made her way upstairs.

"How come you keep going out of town? Is there someone else?" He questioned, gazing her way.

"No. I can't believe you would assume some shit like that Imf. You know I love you and would never do anything to hurt you." Tears started forming in her eyes. "I wouldn't lie to you."

"Word, Ma." He wrapped his arms around her and kissed her forehead. "Shit's just kind of crazy how you always O.T." He stressed. "And never at home."

"What are you suggesting?" She said, looking up at him. *Did he know?*

"Yo, you don't have to dance if you don't want to. I got us, me you, and the baby." He popped her on the ass.

"How did you know?" She looked up at him.

"Last time we fucked you were a little wetter than normal, a little milk squirted in my mouth and I found a pregnancy test in the trash can. When were you gonna tell me?"

"I was gonna wait until the right time," She took a sigh of relief.

"No more secrets, okay?" He kissed her on the forehead.

She nodded her head in agreement.

***

Kesha rode Silk like a Tsunami wave.

"What's my name?" Silk asked as his facial expression varied from the way that Kesha moved with grace against his rock hardness. When she didn't answer, he plunged deeper into her.

"Damn, Imf."

Hold up. What the fuck, Silk thought, reaching back and punching the shit out of Kesha, which caused her to drop to the floor. Kesha went soaring back, hitting her head on the wall. Silk was on his feet.

"What the fuck. I can't believe you called me that nigga." Silk began to kick Kesha in her stomach, side, ass, chest and all her soft spots. Then he picked her up to face him. "I'ma kill you and that nigga," he growled. "I can't believe this shit. How long y'all been fucking?"

"We didn't!" She lied to protect Imf.

"But you thinking about it, you freaky bitch." Silk kicked her to the floor. "Next time you mention me in the same sentence as him, I'ma kill you, Ho."

"I'm sorry," she cried, lying on the floor.

"You got that right." He said before he grabbed his coat and left.

He had to get Imf dealt with. He got into his Range Rover and called up Chocolate Tie.

"Yo. I need that nigga handled, A.S.A.P."

"Word. I got that covered."

* * *

The Gardens was still hotter than lava, but Imf and the crew still managed to somehow keep things up to par by changing spots and switching to a new location not far from the complex they were in. It was only a matter of time before they had things rolling again. Imf grabbed Stacks' keys to his SUV.

"Yo. I'm about to hit the store. Y'all need something?" Imf asked.

"Nah." Everyone said.

"Be right back," Imf said. As he got into Stacks' SUV, his cell rang.
"Yo."

"Imf."

"Who this?" Imf asked, looking at his phone.

"Angie. Imf, you not gon' believe what Silk did to Kesha."

You could see wrinkles on Imf's forehead from the cringe on his face.

"Save that shit and tell me what happen," he impatiently demanded.

"He beat her down like a dog." Angie shook her head as she told him the details.

"Oh he did?" Is all Imf could say. "Where's, Kesha?"

"She right here, but she don't wanna talk."

"Put her on the phone." Angie gave the phone to Kesha. "What he hit you for?" Imf started questioning her.

"I don't know," Kesha cried.

"Don't lie to me!" He shouted.

Don't be mad at me," Kesha cried some more.

"Alright," he said. "I won't be. Just tell me what happened."

"Angie, can you get out?" She asked, wiping her tears. When Angie left the room. Kesha sobbed a little more before she came out with it. "I said your name while we was fucking."

"So he hit you?" Imf asked.

"Yeah, Imf. But it was sort of my fault." she admitted.

"Don't worry. I'ma ride with you regardless. But yo, get you a room for a couple of weeks. I'll pay for that shit until I can get you something better. You listening to me?"

"Yeah," Kesha replied, returning from her thoughts. "Get a room."

"Yeah. And don't leave that mu'fucker until I tell you it's alright."

"Alright," she said before he hung up.

Little did Imf know, but he was being trailed by a black 1994 Cadillac

Deville. He pulled into the B.P. on Silas Creek and went in to purchase some blunts, a brew and some snacks. As Imf made his way out of the service station, he noticed he was being trailed by the Caddy. *A little to close,* he thought, rubbing the stubble up under his chin.

As the Caddy rode up bumping, Imf took caution not even looking in its direction. As soon as he saw the guy in the car mean-mug him and raise his gun, Imf began to let loose. Shots from his 44 Magnum blared out. He could see the driver of the Caddy slumping over in his seat as he drove away from the bloody scene to make his way back to the spot.

"Yo. Some nigga just tried to murder me. I'm sick and tired of this shit!" He vented, after he made it inside.

"It's probably that nigga Trick," Stacks said.

"I told you this shit was crazy. Now you see what I'm talking about," Stacks said to Imf.

"Yeah. You was right." Imf fingered his dreads. "I'm about to ride on everybody in one swoop!" Imf emphasized.

"That's what I'm talking about." Stacks clapped his hands, he was finally about to get some action. There was a knock on the door, so Stacks called down to Big Tank. "Who at the door?"

"A few good smokers. Open up," Big Tank said.

After serving their customers, Imf rounded everyone up and gave them the game plan. Silk was an easy target. They spotted his Range Rover parked downtown.

"Somebody likes to party," Imf said. "Let's catch this nigga in the club so I can crack that nigga upside the head with a bottle of Ace of Spades."

"Nah. Don't waste that kinda money on that fool. Hit that nigga with a bottle of Grey Goose," Hay-Zues added.

When they got inside the club and searched for Silk, he was finally spotted.

"There he go," Hay-Zeus pointed out.

"I'm about to pound this fools head," Imf said, mashing his knuckles into his fist. "Give me that bottle." Imf took the bottle of Grey Goose Hay-Zeus was sippin' on.

Before anyone could see it coming, Imf had come crashing down in Silk's head with the bottle of Grey Goose. Bubbly went everywhere as Imf began beating Silk like a mad man.

"You Bitch! Hit me like you hit Kesha." He scolded, stomping Silk.

After that, all hell broke loose. Hay-Zeus, Stacks, Big Timer and Tank jumped in. When security came, Big Timer and Tank easily man handled them until Imf got his thing off.

"Punk Mu'fucker!" Imf yelled.

He drug Silk outside, and then tossed him head first up against the first thing in sight, which was a Black Rodeo Jeep.

"Hold this mu'fucker," he instructed Hay-Zeus and Stacks. When they restrained him, Imf walked up and smacked Silk like a Wrestler.

"Don't you ever fucking hit Kesha again. Do you understand?"

Silk Nodded in agreement.

"Good. Now put that nigga down on his face." Once they did, Imf called Tank and Big Timer over. "Jump on that niggas hands. Break every one of his fingers to make sure he learns how to treat a woman," he instructed as he walked off.

He could see Stacks and Hay-Zeus holding Silk down while Big Timer and Tank jumped on his hands like a trampoline. *We served that mo'fucker well,* Imf thought. Now all he had to do was find Trick's bitch ass. *That couldn't be so hard,* he thought.

Imf and his men were slumped down in a smoked out Caddy watching the numerous crack heads floating up and down Trick's spot.

"Yo," Imf called out to one of his so called customers.

"What up?" Shakes approached the window, bobbing from side to side, which explains exactly why they called him shakes.

"Yo, who got some coke around here?" Imf already knew the answer, but played it off.

"Trick and his boys got this shit on lock around here. A yo, Imf. I was thinking," he said as he started nodding off.

"What's that?" Imf asked.

"Let me get a bag of that boy to go along with this girl," he held up a bag of white dust.

"Get that shit out of here," Imf looked around for the cops.

"What's wrong?" Shakes began to shake worse than ever.

"Twenty-five to life, stupid mu'fucker," Imf frowned. "Get the hell away from the car." Imf was starting to get frustrated. "Fuck it. Let's go up in there and let God sort 'em out." Imf squeezed his 44 Magnum tight. The crew got out and made their way up the crowded staircase.

"Yo, who goes there?" One of Trick's cocky lookout men asked.

"Me," Imf pulled the trigger, piercing a single bullet into Trick's man's skull, sending him to his destiny. "Y'all wanna fuck with Imf, so now y'all gon' feel my fucking rage."

He and his men began busting their guns on sight. Trick's men were trying to do all they could, but their fire power was no match for all the heavy artillery they were up against. Needless to say, bodies got dropped and heads got cracked, and yet and still there was no Trick. Imf made his way into the spot were Trick hustled. He busted in and sent one shot into Joe-Joe's head, and then he looked at Rufus.

"Tell me were Trick is, or you're next." He pointed the gun.

"I'm loyal, fool. Kill me." Rufus played tough.

"Boom." Was all that was heard.

"Let's be out," Imf mentioned, shortly after dropping Rufus' stupid ass.

***

Trick was over Amber's house when everything went down, so he had no clue that his spot was getting ambushed. When he got that phone call, he sat up in bed.

"Is everything okay?" Amber sat beside him.

"No." He hushed her with a cold stare. "Word." He took a deep sigh. It was Imf's punk ass again.

"Yeah. Stay on the low," Duke told him.

"You ain't gotta tell me twice," he exclaimed. Trick's started thinking of ways to make money while not being on the scene. Imf's punk ass had killed about ten of his men, but that still left him with about twelve loyal soldiers, a bunch of young niggas who would ride and die cause they loved him. All he had to do was take them to the mall to buy them a few kicks and outfits. In return, they would do whatever he asked. He wanted to get them to off Imf so badly, but he knew that wish was highly impossible. He knew a war was the last thing he wanted with Imf. Trick knew it was best to let by gones be by gones and just continue to get money. It took money to infiltrate a war, and that was something he barely had. Now he wished he hadn't been tricking so much.

"Is everything okay, Trick?"

"Yeah Ma. It is now." He kissed her. "I'm gonna need to use your house for a little while."

"Cool. Just make sure you don't get my shit ran into," Amber said.

"The only thing that's getting ran in to is you." He straddled on top of her, parted her legs and entered her hole. "I'm about to nut all in this shit," he said as he plunged into her raw dog.

Amber didn't stop him. She was in love with Trick. The way he thrust into her almost drove her crazy. She couldn't wait until the right time to tell him that she having his child. She arched her back as he dove in and out of her.

"Uh-uh. That's feels so good," she cooed.

"I don't want nobody in this pussy but me. You understand." He rammed into her. "This my pussy. Understand?"

"Yeah, yeah. I understand," she moaned. "Now make it cum for me."

He fucked her with aggression, fucked her for his niggas who were dead and no longer here, fucked her cause he was a trick, nothing more and nothing less.

***

Imf woke up in the comfort of Kesha's arms.

"Yo. What up, Baby?"

"Thank you so much!" She squeezed his neck.

"For what?" He asked, looking into her eyes.

"For getting Silk out my life. I'm ready to start brand new. I wanna learn how to cook up coke, and I really wanna help you lock things down."

"Hold on, Imf sat up." He rubbed the sleep from his face. "Shit. Did I tell you I got a baby on the way?"

"What?" She twisted her face up in a snarl.

"Yeah, but that was before, you know," Imf rubbed his head.

"Yeah. I know. So who is it? I don't know if I can put up with Alexia."

"Kesh, he held her hand. It's not by Alexia."

She looked at him with a curious expression.

"Imf, you better not tell me you had a baby by that bitch I don't like."
Imf was quiet, he didn't know what or how to say it was.

"It is." She finally said. "I can't believe this," she huffed. "Imf, I really loved you. I mean, I really thought we could build a foundation together."

"And who said we can't? Look I put everything out on the table."

"Right, so where do we go from here?" She asked.

"We don't go nowhere unless you feel like the need to leave." He laid back in bed. "I really love you, Kesh, and I can't make it without you in my life."

"So, what are you saying?" She replied, looking at him.

"I ain't saying shit. I'm asking that you do your best so we can work it out."

"I'll try," she said, crawling on Imf. He was about to say something when she quieted him by placing her finger over his lips. "Make love to me."

"I got some condoms in my pocket," he told her.

"Don't worry about it. I wanna feel you." She inserted him into her.

She began to move in a slow pace. It was like Imf's dick knew how to make her happy and definitely how to make her pussy overjoyed. Kesha knew without a doubt that this was where she wanted to be. She loved to be on top of, beside or just around a nigga of his caliber. She thought about his current girlfriend, and didn't like that bitch. And the fact that she was having a baby by Imf before Kesha, cut her deeply. She rode Imf hard with hopes of conceiving his child. After hours of love making, Imf hugged Kesha and they sat in bed quietly thinking.

"What you thinking?" She looked up at Imf.

"About life just like you." He graced her face with his hand.

"I always wondered what it would be like to be with you."

"Now you know." She snickered.

"Shut up," he responded, kissing her. "But yo. About that cooking thing. That shit is cool, but I think I need you to hold me down by going another route."

"Like what, Imf?" She asked, looking up at him in dismay.

"I need you to be the legitimate one out of the crew." He hugged her. "You my super star."

"What do you need me to do?" She questioned as she nibbled along his neck.

"What?" He asked, smiling. "You tickling the shit out of me."

"So. Tough guy."

"You listening," he responded and turned his neck to the side.

"Yeah. I'm listening, Imf." She huffed and rolled her eyes.

"Good. Cause without you, shit ain't gon' work."

"What are you talking about?"

"You the one that connects everything together."

"I'm not understanding you."

"But pretty soon you will. Look I need you to go back to school and find something, anything that you wanna do and do it."

"I don't have that type of money," she frowned.

"I got you," he assured her. "First thing in the morning, I want you to go get us a place and lay our house out," Imf told her.

"Is that it?" She peered up at him.

"For right now," he said.

"What's wrong?" Kesha rubbed Imf's worried face.

Seemed like everything Imf never told anyone, he was willing to share with Kesha.

"I feel like the Fed's are on me."

"Oh, Imf." It's probably all that weed you smoke," she said, brushing his dreads to the side to kiss him.

"Yeah, you probably right," he said.

"Let's go take a shower so I can do something big with you."

Imf got out of bed with his dick swaying from side to side. He and Kesha got in the shower. He washed her up and she did the same in return.

Then she bent down and wrapped her mouth around his pipe and began to suck him. Afterwards, he returned the favor. Imf sucked Kesha until her knees buckled and she collapsed against the shower. He got up slowly and made his way inside of her from the back. Rubbing her erect nipples with his hand, he parted her pussy to play in it. Kesha rotated her hips and arched her back as he cocked her leg up and gave it to her rough, just like she loved it.

After Imf got finished stretching Kesha out, he got a call from his connect Panama, informing him that he was in town and needed to see him A.S.A.P. Without hesitation, Imf got Kesha to take him to the arranged spot. Imf got out the car while Kesha waited.

Little did Imf and Panama know, they were being watched by the FED's and D.E.A. Panama introduced Imf to a guy who wanted to buy a large quantity of coke. Imf wasn't too fond of Panama introducing him to a guy he'd never met, so he thought it was suspicious.

Imf ran his fingers though his goatee.

"What's his name?" He asked Panama, skeptical.

"Jeff." Panama replied.

"I don't trust him," Imf gritted. "He looks like a cop. You the police?" Imf inquired.

"Hell nah!" Jeff lied. "What's up with your manz?" Jeff looked at Panama.

"He's cool, Imf. The guys straight up." Panama ripped Jeff's clothes off to search him.

"See," Jeff swallowed. He was scared as shit, hoping that no one would check his cellular that had a wire inside the head piece. "I told you I wasn't the fucking Po-Po," Jeff responded.

"Shut up," Imf threatened. "Yo, Panama, let me holler at you," Imf nodded in his direction, moving out of ears reach.

"Sup Man?"

"Yo, I don't trust this guy as far as I can throw him."

Panama was thinking the same thing, but didn't verbalize it.

"You asked him if was he a cop and he told you no. They gotta tell you if they really are, or that's entrapment. Right?"

"Exactly," Imf replied.

"So what do you think? This is your boy, correct."

"I think you should get him to meet you on your stomping grounds and make this million dollar deal for us," Panama stated.

Imf took a deep sigh, because he had a funny feeling about all this.

"Just like that?"

"Just like that," responded Panama. "You in or what?"

"Yeah, but give me til about ten tonight, and on my terms." Imf left.

* * *

I knew damn well I wasn't feeling this deal that Panama hooked up. Money was the root to all evil and greed was a mu'fucker. I was thinking make this deal and leave the game. Would this be my last deal or what? My heart beat like I was hooked up to a cardio accelerator machine, Imf thought.

Kesha's voluptuous body laid across the Hotel bed. Imf had fucked her real good just in case it was his last time. He cocked his 45., placing it behind his back as he heard a horn blowing. He knew it was Big Timer and Tank. He kissed Kesha and left out of the room, hopping into the SUV that awaited. He sat back reflecting on his life. *I'm twenty-seven with one kid, didn't finish school and have killed. Lord knows how many people. Maybe if this deal goes through, I'll get legit and go to school or something. Nah. Who am I fooling? I love this game because it doesn't take too much intelligence, and anyone can do it.*

The smart man stacked his chips and got out the game fast, but the greedy man stuffed his face until he couldn't eat anymore. I'm saying that to say this.

Imf pulled up to the vacant warehouse, Stacks and Hay-Zeus were located at the top of the building with enough dynamite to blow up the World Trade Center, and enough fire power to fight against the Taliban. Ten minutes later, a white limo pulled up and Jeff got out. Imf really didn't care too much for this fool, but he carried on with the plan.

"You got that?" Jeff asked.

"No talking. I ask all the questions. You the police?" Imf double checked. "You know you gotta tell me."

And blow my cover, Jeff thought.

"The same ole shit." Jeff waved his arms, realizing that was the wrong move because Imf's men were waving their guns with the infrared at his head.

"Check this fool out." Imf instructed. With the wave of a hand, Imf's men moved in and thoroughly frisked Jeff down.

"I told you I wasn't a cop for the last time." Jeff assured.

"Where the money?" Imf asked.

"Where the Product?" Jeff asked. "I don't got all day."

"You got until I say you do." I'mf gritted.

Something wasn't right with this guy. It's almost like this guy is challenging me, or like we're fucking the same bitch, Nah, Imf quickly erased those assumptions out of his head. *This nigga could never pull a bitch like the ones I fucked with, cause he's got too much bitch in him. Just a soft and mushy dude.*

"You don't like me do you?" Jeff asked.

"Hell no!" Imf told the truth, waving for Big Timer to grab the brief case out the ride.

"The feelings neutral," Jeff shot back. "What you gon' do with my money?"

"Buy you some game, so you can get some pussy." Imf glared at Jeff.

"I get plenty." Jeff smirked, thinking, *But you won't when you sitting back rotting in someone's pen.*

"Yeah right." Imf spat, as he held the briefcase Big Timer gave him. "The money."

Jeff smirked as he wrapped up his thoughts about giving Imf time that reflected top NFL numbers, *10 to 20, maybe 30 to life.*

"Yeah. Right this way." Jeff nodded to the trunk of the limo. He grabbed a briefcase filled with money and tossed it to Imf. "Here, it's all there."

"I'll be the indicator of that," Imf inspected the money. As he was about to step off, Jeff stopped him in the process.

"Yo, the shit."

"Oh yeah. I almost forgot. But just to make sure, I'ma asked you again, you ain't no cop, right?"

"Hell no!" Jeff was fuming.

His yellowish skin began to alternate to a reddish color, and his blood began to bubble with anger.

"Good. Cause I'll call you back with information on where you can pick the shit up from." Imf tossed Jeff an empty brief case.

Jeff stared at the empty brief case blankly. This kid Imf was smarter than he thought. Had he sold him the product, the FED's would've been outside waiting on him. He glared at him as he left like he was the replica of Nino Brown. *Damn clown*, he thought. The movie I'm gonna get you sucker played in his head, because that's exactly what he was planning to do to Imf before it was all over and done with.

Imf left the warehouse and gave Jeff the instructions on where he could pick up the work.

"We rich baby," he told the crew as they made sure they wasn't being trailed by any police, D.E.A. or the FEDs.

Jeff pulled up to the curb, Imf was smarter than he thought, *Where was this mu'fucker.* Jeff waited and waited, but no one came. That's when it dawned on him that he had got played. What was he going to tell his Supervisor and Director about the million dollars that he was unaccountable for. He had some serious matters to take care of.

His first stop was to Maliah's crib, hoping that Imf was there. He was gonna kill that son-of-a-bitch. He got to Maliah's crib and damn near beat down her door.

"You wanna us to come in with you?" His partners asked.

"No. Let me handle this." Jeff replied.

When the door opened, Jeff presented a search warrant then stepped into the house with his gun drawn. "What are you doing walking in my damn house like you crazy?" Maliah covered her exposed body with her robe.

"Where is he?" Jeff growled.

"Where's who?" Maliah played dumb.

"Ingram Washington formally known as Prince, Bitch! That's who?" Jeff raised his tone in anger.

"What do you want him for?" Maliah wanted to know. "Is this one of your games? Oh let me guess. This is supposed to be some kind of dick swinging contest?" She shouted.

Jeff looked at her.

"He does things for me you just can't do." She spoke her mind.

"We'll see about that when the both of you are doing time. Get dressed, Bitch. You going down to the station."

* * *

Maliah sat at a table in the interrogation room in handcuffs. Her head was pounding. She was so worried about Imf that she had been crying. She wondered if he was safe and if he would get much time or not. Maliah only wanted what was best for Imf. As she sniffled in tears, her supervisor walked in.

"Maliah," he placed his hand on her shoulder. "I know you're innocent of the crimes against you."

"I am," Maliah said. "I don't know what this is all about."

"Oh you know." Her superior, who resembled the actor, Harrison Ford said. "But I'm willing to give you a second chance if you help us take this guy down. He stole money from the government, and he deserves a 95 percent conviction rate just because we can do whatever we fucking feel like to his bitch ass."

Maliah looked at him blankly. "Fire me. I will not be a part of anything that isn't right."

"What's not right is you sleeping with a well known Drug Lord and your one of my best Agents."

"I won't do it!" She shouted. "So whatever you have to do, do it without me," she cried as tears filled her eyes.

"You're so much better than this guy." He looked at her. "I trust that you will make the right choice. I would love for you to remain with the government."

"I won't be a part of this. What do expect me to do?" She cried. "He is the father of my child."

"Sorry to hear that," he took a half sigh. In ways he couldn't explain, he had sympathy for Maliah. "You're a smart lady. Get the father of your child the best possible deal you can. Right now we have his ass on a shit load of charges." He waved Jeff in.

"I'll let you two talk," he suggested before he left Maliah and Jeff alone.

"Looks like someone's all tied up," Jeff said, walking in with a slight smirk upon his face. He glanced at the handcuffs. "I never thought it would be you."

"What is this about, me not fucking you." She spat.

"Believe me. The pussy ain't the bomb like you think. Tell me, what did that no good mu'fucker do that I didn't." Jeff questioned.

"So this is about you wanting me."

"Maybe it is, so answer to my question."

"Trust me, you don't wanna know."

"Try me." Jeff rubbed his chin.

Maliah wanted Jeff to hurt and suffer like she did.

"He eats my pussy. Tosses my salad like a master chef and blows out by brains like he's a trained assassin. Something you can't even come close to doing," she truthfully informed him.

"Is he bigger than me?" Jeff was curious.

"You don't wanna know," she slightly turned her head.

"Answer me," Jeff demanded, roughly turning her head to look at him.

"It doesn't matter."

"Is he bigger than me or is he thicker?" Jeff asked.

"Both," she glared at him in disgust. "After he gave it to me, you didn't have a chance."

Jeff was crushed.

"Well, I'm not the one who needs the chance. You do," he snickered. "Check out this evidence against Mr. Washington," he leaned towards her to show her a picture of Panama. "You know him?"

"Yeah. That's the guy we've been building a case on for the last ten years, but could never catch him." She said.

"Yeah. Now look at this." Jeff placed the pictures of Imf with the Notorious Drug Lord better known as Panama. "Your boy is fucked." To make matters worse, Jeff went over and cut the T.V. on. "We purchased some coke from this guy." Jeff lied. "See the transaction." Jeff zoomed in and kept pressing replay. "See the hand off."

Jeff played the whole video of what was supposed to be a controlled buy. Imf and his low budget hooligans had only run off with a million in cash, so Jeff knew he had nothing on Imf but a potential tampering with evidence case.

"I need your help. You help me. I'll help you and you help Imf," he told her. "Or," he sighed. "He's gonna spend the rest of his natural born life in prison, then you'll be raising this child all alone." Jeff said.

"Is this because I won't be with you?" She cried.

"This is never personal. Do you want me to make this light on Imf, or do you want me to make it hard on you?" Jeff asked.

"How much time is he facing?"

"That depends on you," replied Jeff. "We don't really want Imf. He's a low life street nigga with no class. We want his supplier. If you can convince Imf to turn Panama in. You'll get to keep this good government job, save your family and hopefully Imf won't go to jail." Jeff lied. "Think about it," he went up to her and rubbed her face.

All Maliah could do at that moment was shed tears and think about Imf's best interest. She loved him and didn't want the father of her unborn child to be in prison. So she did what any woman that was crazy in love would do for their man. She decided to cop a deal with Jeff and try to convince Imf to testify against Panama.

Chapter: Nine

Cause those lips, those eyes love the way that you look at me baby!
Those hips, those thighs love the way you fuck me baby, by Ja Rule played
as Imf pulled up to Winston Salem State College. This was the home of the
Rams, and Imf was there to pick up his Boo Kesha. She had gotten enrolled
in school and was taking things more serious then he thought.

A lot had changed since he had pulled off the caper with Jeff and for
some reason he couldn't convince himself that Jeff wasn't a cop. The more
he tried to convince himself of that shit, the more money he spent on
material shit. Not only had he paid for Kesha's schooling with hopes that
one day it would pay off in the long run, but he had copped a condo for
them, schooled her on every aspect of the game just in case, and even
showed her how to cook up. He'd stopped her from hustling slightly,
because she still had her certain people she dealt with. The girl was a true
hustler. He just hoped she'd bust her ass on the school shit like she did with
the coke game. He arrived at the front entrance of the building her class was
in and waited on Kesha. as Ja Rule continued to bumped.

That's what I'm talking about, Imf thought as Kesha and everyone else
at her school looked at his fat ass new ride. His all black Knight XV, damn
near five hundred thousand dollar armored vehicle made a statement.

"Gurl. Who is that?" Shaneaka asked Kesha. "Your guess is as good as
mines," Kesha replied.

"He's blasting that Ashanti and Ja Rule. Let's go holler," Shaneka said.

"I'm not going over there. I'm waiting on my man to come pick me
up."

"You're no fun. I'm about to go holler," Shaneaka replied.

"Go head."

Shaneaka and Kesha met one day while applying for college. They weren't real cool, cause Kesha could judge a gutter rat when she saw one. She couldn't blame her for trying her hand with whoever was in that fat ass ride.

Damn. Where's Imf. She thought, as she saw Shaneaka go up to the all black tinted up SUV.

She watched Shaneaka frown and get upset.

"Your lost," she said before she stepped off.

He must've really shut her down cold, Kesha figured as she waited. Suddenly, the SUV pulled up in front of her.

"Yo," Imf stepped out. "You tryna set a nigga by sending bitches at me?" He held his arms out and wrapped them around her.

"No. Hell no!" Kesha said, smiling as everyone looked at them. "If I knew that bitch was try'na get at you, I would've whooped that heffah's ass. Hold up, Imf! What's up with the Jeep?"

"What's up?"He looked back. "That shits fat right?"

"Yeah. But," she half said.

"But what?"

"How much did it cost?"

"Hella grip, but money ain't a thing."

"Imf, how much did you spend on it?"

"A little under a mill."

Kesha's mouth dropped.

"Imf. Are you crazy? Why did you spend that much money on a damn Jeep?" She asked ballistic.

"Let's talk about this later," Imf looked around. He felt as if he was being followed. "Come on, get in." Kesha was all frowned up. "You know you like it." Imf said, getting into the ride.

"But I don't understand why you went and bought the most expensive whip on the market." She crossed her arms and looked at him.

"For security reasons."

"Yeah right. Ain't nobody in their right mind crazy enough to mess with you."

"I got money now," he told her.

"I see," she retorted. "So that's your reason for the whip?"

"No. I feel like mu'fucker's out to get me and take everything I've worked so hard for," he responded, interrupted by a phone call.

"Yo."

"How did everything go?" Panama asked.

"We took that sucker for everything he had. You should've seen his face." Imf teased.

"Imf, I know you ain't stick ole boy up?" Panama got serious.

"Then you know wrong." Imf informed him.

"That's not how we conduct business." Panama told Imf.

"You'll thank me later. In the meantime, I got your half. So what you want me to do with it? Imf asked.

"Hold it." Panama started thinking. "So you think this guy was police?"

"No doubt."

"You think this will come back to haunt us?"

"Yeah, but until then I'm gon' party like every day is my last."

"Word. Well you know how to get in touch with me if you need me? Is everything steady?" His words for needing more coke.

"I'm good. It's plenty."

"Good, because I'm about to go out of town for a while."

'Don't get scared now. You wasn't scared when you introduced me to Jeff's uppity ass."

"That may have been a bad move, and one that could cost me."

"Don't slip or trip. I ain't no rat," Imf told him.

Good. Panama thought because he knew when the boat caught on fire the rat's jumped overboard while the ship sank.

"Just be careful,"

"I always do," Imf said before hanging up. He looked over and Kesha was staring at him clear as day. "What up?"

"Who did you sell too?"

"Damn, you nosy."

"I should be. You my man," she shoved Imf's arm.

Imf told Kesha about how him and his crew robbed the potential informant. As well as about the need for the full proof armored SUV.

"Now you understand why I'm so worried," he took a deep sigh.

"Yeah, Imf. I just wish you wouldn't have sold to that guy," she said.

"Yeah, me too," he said as he drove off. "But yo, I gotta drop you off at the house while I go take care of a few things."

"You always try'na drop somebody off at the house," she complained.

"Yeah, you need to be on some cook and clean up the house type of shit,"

"You got it twisted. If you hungry then you better stop somewhere and get something to eat. One thing you should know about me by now is that when I get home, I'm about making some money."

"Oh it's like that?"

"Exactly," she smirked.

Imf picked up some food, and then pulled up in front of their new condo

"Let your boy get some of them sexy lips before I go."

Kesha leaned over and placed a kiss on Imf's lips.

"Hurry back home so I can get some," she said with a devilish grin on her face.

"We can get it in right now." Imf suggested.

"No. I don't do quickies. You gotta take your time and do it right," she teased, stepping out of the SUV. "Like I know you can," she walked off.

Imf squeezed his dick. He debated whether to catch up with Kesha now or later. He pulled off bumping, "Minds Playing Tricks on Me" by the Ghetto Boys. He made sure to keep his eyes on the rear view mirror. He wiped the sweat that trickled down his forehead. Maybe he was noided out cause he could've sworn he was being trailed.

Silk was furious as he and his boys trailed Imf. As soon as Imf stopped at the light, Silk and his men jumped out.

What the fuck. Imf thought. As four figures crept up to his SUV and started firing, Imf ducked.

"Oh shit!" He said as he watched a nigga come up to his door and point the gun to his head.

"Take this mu'fucker."

As the gunman fired, bullets bounced off the windshield. The gunman grabbed for the handle of the door and was shocked so bad that he dropped to the ground and shook like he was having convulsions.

Imf did some quick thinking and pressed a button on the stirring wheel that blew out purple smoke and had everyone wheezing like Wheezy baby. After creating a diversion, he pulled off. He was furious that someone tried to take his life. It could only be one person. Trick's bitch ass. Imf drove to the PJ's and called his boys. The other matter that he had to take care of could be taken up later. But right now he had to kill Trick. He scooped up his boys and they went looking for Trick.

They were out asking crackheads if they had seen him, but no one had seen or heard from him in the past few days.

***

"Trick," Amber said, wrapping her arms around his neck.

"What up, Ma?" Trick palmed her plump ass. "You know what I wanna do?" Trick pressed her up against his hardness.

"I have something to tell you," she informed him.

"Tell me later." Trick kissed her like nothing or no one else mattered. He made love to her. Afterwards, he flopped on the couch after unloading twice. *Damn Amber got some good ass pussy,* he thought to himself. "So what did you have to tell me?" He asked as he wrapped his arm around her.

"I'm pregnant," she smiled.

"By who?" Trick played stupid. "Not by me."

"But," her smile turned to a frown of sadness.

"But shit." Trick got off the sofa. "That little mu'fucker ain't mines. Who you been fucking?" He snapped.

"You and only you." She swore, looking at him. "Trick, I love you," she told him as she tried to wrap her arms around his neck, which is when he pushed her back.

"Shit. I ain't ready to be no daddy. Hell I'm a kid myself."

"We'll get through this," she told him, cupping his face in the palms of her hands.

"No. You'll get through it!" Trick snapped before he walked out the door.

Just as quick as Trick walked into her life, he walked out. Amber wasn't having it. She ran after him hooting and hollering.

"What about our baby?" She said as everyone in the projects stared at her like she had lost her damn mind.

"Fuck you bitch! You ain't nothing but a crackhead." Trick yelled, continuing to ignore her.

Swear to God that shit hurt. Amber watched as Trick walked out of her life. She knew how to fix his ass. She'd heard that someone was looking for

119

Trick and she wanted something terrible to happen to him. She made her way to Imf's complex where she was approached by Tank.

"Yo. What you want?"

"I need to see Imf." She cried.

"You can't. Now tell me what's wrong." Tank comforted her.

She told Tank about all that had transpired. Without question Tank led her to Imf who listened patiently.

"So what you're telling me is that Trick got you pregnant and said he wasn't the daddy. Man, get her some tissue," Imf directed Tank.

Amber wiped her tears with the Kleenex and nodded her head in agreement.

"So what you want me to do?" Imf asked.

"Kill his no good ass."

"All you gotta do is tell me where he be." Imf assured.

***

"My roll." Trick said, as he slung dice in the project hallways. He had no idea what was about to transpire.

"Yo." Doser Boy looked up. "Y'all hear that?" He asked.

"No, you trippin'," Pike said.

"Nah. I know I ain't trippin'," Doser said, with his ears sticking up like a bloodhound.

Out of nowhere figures approached. No words were uttered, just the sound of shots from deadly assault rifles. Everyone took flight. Some weren't so lucky. Trick wasn't one of them, he was able to take off. Word to life, he was so scared, he ran faster than Usain Bolt on the Jamaican Sprint team.

Stacks' was on Trick's trail until he juked a move that was so slick that Stacks' momentarily lost him. *Damn, that nigga faster than a crackhead*, he thought to himself.

What would you do if you had wolves on you? Trick did what nine out of ten of the average nigga's who didn't want no problems did. He went to some nigga's who could help him. He ran up in the police station so fast, he almost knocked the doors off the hinges.

"So let me get this right. You want Ingram Washington arrested. Why?" asked the detective.

"Cause him and his crew where shooting at me, and I think he killed Tray Duce." Trick said as if the detective knew who Tray Duce was.

"Who is Tray Duce?"

"The young kid they found dead in the projects," Trick couldn't stop talking.

"Could you please slow down?" asked the detective.

"Yeah." Trick took a deep sigh then began again, but this time he was talking even faster than before. He told the police everything. Where they could find Imf and everything. "And I put that on my moms." Trick told the detective when he finished.

The police was forced to take action. They ran up in Happy Hill projects with the S.W.A.T. team, helicopters and all. They went door to door asking around for Imf after ransacking his drug spot. Lucky for him he wasn't around.

* * *

Imf was at the crib with Kesha.

"Damn you fine," Imf said as he caressed Kesha's chocolate toned body.

Nothing could get him out of his zone. Almost nothing until his cell began to chirp.

"Don't get that." She grabbed at his hand.

"It might be important," he told her as he reached for his cell.

121

While he talked, Kesha never lost a beat. She went down to unbuckle his pants, kissing all along his torso. Damn, was she about to bless a nigga with some head. Soon as Kesha took him in like ice cream, Imf's conversation grew in excitement. The disturbing news he got caused him to removed her head.

"What you do that for," Kesha snapped, frowning.

"What?" he said to Big Timer, holding his finger up for her to stop.

"Police are everywhere, and they are looking for you. They got a search warrant," Big Timer anxiously told him.

Imf took a deep sigh. He was at a lost for words. He always knew that his fate would come to an end in this game that wasn't designed for winners.

He felt as if his heart had just jumped out his chest.

"What's wrong?" Kesha asked concerned.

"Nothing," he said, coming out of deep thought. "But yo. I gotta go," he told Big Timer.

As soon as he hung up he got an unsuspected call.

"Yo."

"Imf," Maliah wiped the tears from her face.

"Yo, what's up?" He asked with concern.

"I need to talk to you."

"Cool. I'll be there in a minute."

It never dawned on him that he hadn't heard from Maliah in some time. All he knew was he needed to go check on the mother of his unborn child. He got up from the bed and fastened his pants.

"Where you going?" Kesha questioned, trailing behind him.

"I gotta go handle something," he told her.

"Imf, I'm worried don't go," she pleaded as tears escaped from her eyes.

"I love you," Imf told her as he wiped her tears and kissed her lips.

"I know," she wrapped her arms around him. "Don't go."

"I have to. I gotta go check on my baby momma."

"Alexia," she asked.

"Nah."

"Oh," she looked down. "I am so jealous that she has a kid by you."

"Don't be," he kissed her forehead. "I love you."

"I know." She responded, taking her hands from around him. "I'll be waiting for you with no clothes on." She walked back over to the bed. "So hurry back."

With that Imf bounced to go see what was wrong with Maliah. She had been let out of the holding tank after being locked up for at least a week. She had stopped counting. All she could think about was helping Imf get out all of the trouble he was in.

"You look like shit." Jeff told her.

"Fuck you!" She spat. "The only reason I'll do this is if you agree to let Imf off on all charges." She glared at Jeff.

"Only if you convince him to take the stand on Panama," Jeff replied, playing hard ball.

He wanted Imf worse than Panama for sticking him up for the million in cash. *But Panama will do for now*, he thought.

Maliah was let out of jail and rehired all in the same day. She only had time to eat and take a nice hot bath before she heard Imf using his key to get in. She ran down stairs and ran into his embrace.

"Damn. Somebody happy to see me," he teased. "Always," she   smiled, wiping her tears.

"Damn. You lose some weight?" He asked, looking at her.

"A little," she whimpered.

Now she wished that she had eaten a little better while she had been in lockup.

"Don't be starving my seed." He rubbed her belly.

"I won't," she smiled.

"Why you crying?"

"I don't know," she shrugged. Just happy to see you." She told him. "Let's go upstairs."

"What?"

"You heard me," Maliah said, letting her robe fall to the floor.

Imf squeezed his dick as he watched Maliah's heavenly figure sway up the steps.

"Now I remember why I fell in love with you."

Maliah smiled. She had to be a good actor cause she wanted to cry for what she was about to do. Imf let his pants drop as soon as he reached the top step. He made his way in the room and wasted no time. He caressed Maliah's honey brown tits as he devoured her with kisses. She leaned back as he placed kisses along her neck down to her breast.

"Oh God!" She called out.

"The best is yet to come," he told her, as he positioned her on the edge of the bed. She arched back and Imf straddled her. He swiped her down there and made sure she was ready. Her juices were dripping from his hand. "Damn, I got you gushing," he cocked her legs open and entered her residence. Imf continued making love to Maliah and when it was all said and done, he rested back on the pillow, noticing Maliah was teary eyed. "What's wrong?" Imf asked.

"Imf, I love you," Maliah sobbed. She rubbed his face. "Don't ever think I don't."

"Where that shit come from?" He looked up, but before he could get the question out. Maliah had pulled out some handcuffs and placed them around both risk.

"What the fuck?" He said as Maliah kissed him on the cheek.

It was then that his whole life went into a blur.

"You're under arrest. Anything you say can and will be used against you in the court of law," she said, reading him his rights. A bunch of F.B.I. and D.E.A. agents busted into the room, pointing guns at Imf.

Can you believe this shit? Imf thought.

Kesha waited in bed for Imf to return home. She waited and waited and waited until she drifted off to sleep. She had no idea that Imf was handcuffed and on his was to an interrogation room.

* * *

As Imf sat at the table in the interviewing room, Maliah walked in.

"So you're a cop?" He asked.

"Yeah." She answered, taking a seat in front of him.

"I never would've thought."Imf chuckled.

"Imf I'm doing this for us. You, me and the baby," she told him.

Imf made a nasty noise right before he spit in Maliah's face.

"That fucking bastard ain't mine!"

Maliah wiped her face of his saliva.

"I can understand you being mad," she acknowledged as Imf spit on her again.

"Bitch, if I ever see you again, I'll kill you!" He snapped.

"Maliah, are you alright?" Jeff stepped into the room.

"Yeah," she responded, wiping the spit from her face. "Listen," she told Imf. "I'm try'na help you."

"How Bitch? By locking a nigga up?"

"It wasn't meant to happen like this," she shook her head.

"All you gotta do is take a stand," Jeff intervened.

"So." Imf smiled. "Now I know why you didn't like me. I told myself that we couldn't have fucked the same bitch, but I guess I was wrong," he commented, looking at Maliah.

"lmf, I made a deal for you so we can go off and raise this child. All you have to do is testify against Panama and they'll let you go scott free.   What do you say?" She asked.

Flashes of Mr. Biggs song, 'I started selling dope back in 1986. I bought a Caddy and some rims and put some things all around it,' played in Imf mind. He smirked, leaned back in his seat, and then responded.

"I think we gone take this shit to trail," stated Imf.

Shit was unfinished. He knew this was war and the war had only just gotten started. Word, this shit ain't over.

To be continued…

Quick Order Form

To Order:

Go to Createspace or Amazon.com

Please send the following book(s):

___ Get It In

U$11.99. + Shipping

Shipping To:

Name:_____

Address:_____

City:_____State:_____Zip:_____

We Help You Self-Publish Your Book

Crystell Publications has worked hard to build our quality brand. Regardless of your status, our team will help you get to print. Our BLOW OUT prices are for serious authors only. And surely with fees like these, every author who desires to be published can. **Don't have all your money? .... No Problem!** *Ask About our Payment Plans*

Crystal Perkins-Stell, MHR
Essence Magazine Bestseller
We Give You Books!
PO BOX 8044 / Edmond – OK 73083
www.crystalstell.com
(405) 414-3991

Our competitor's Cheapest Plans- **AuthorHouse** Legacy Plan $1299.00- 8 books **Xilibris** Professional Plan $1249.00 10 bks, **iUniverse** Premier Plan $1299.00-5 bks
Hey! Stop Wishing, and get your book to print NOW!!!

–Recession Big Flex Options 100 Books–					
Option A	**Option B**	**Option C**	**Option D**	**E-Book**	**Option F**
$1399.00	$1299.00	$1199.00	$839.00	$695.00	$775.00
255-275	205-250	200 -80	75 - 60	255 pages	50 or less

Grind Plans 25 & E-Book	**Hustle Hard**	**Respect The Code**	**313 Deal**
Order Extra Books	$899.00	$869.00	$839.00
	255-275pg	250 -205	200 -80

Insanity Plans 2 Books & E-Book & POD	**Psycho**	**Spastic**	**Mental**
Extra Books Can Be Ordered	$759.00	$659.00	$559.00
	225-250pg	200-220	199- 100

All Manuscript Options except the E-Books include:
2 Proofs –Publisher & Printer Copy, Mink Magazine Subscription, Free Advertisement, Book Cover, ISBN #, Conversion, Typeset, Correspondence, Masters, 8 hrs Consultation

$100.00 E-book upload only
$275.00-Book covers/Authors input
$269.00-Book covers/ templates
$190.00 and up Websites
$375.00, book trailers on Youtube

$75 Can't afford edits, Spell-check
$499 Flat Rate Edits Exceeds 210 add 1.50 pp
$200-Typeset Book Format PDF File
$200 and up / Type Manuscript Call for details

We're Killing The Game.

No more paying Vanity Presses $8 to $10 per book! We Give You Books @ Cost. **We Offer Editing For An Extra Fee- If Waved, We Print What You Submit!** These titles are done by self-published authors. They are not published by nor signed to Crystell Publications.

128